Sophie Dickinson was born and raised in the beautiful countryside of Pembrokeshire. From a young age, she always had a great passion for writing. At age 12, Sophie entered into a competition for young writers, to later have a poem published in *The Poetry Games*. Her ambition in life is to inspire her readers and take them through a journey into a different types of reality. In her leisure time, she enjoys variable sports and music.

S.Dickinson

Sophie Dickinson

DARK LIES

AUSTIN MACAULEY PUBLISHERS™

LONDON • CAMBRIDGE • NEW YORK • SHARJAH

A CIP catalogue record for this title is available from the British Library.

ISBN 9781398413504 (Paperback)
ISBN 9781398494008 (ePub e-book)

www.austinmacauley.com

First Published 2022
Austin Macauley Publishers Ltd®
1 Canada Square
Canary Wharf
London
E14 5AA

Chapter One
At the Beginning's End

I held his fragile body in mine, his skin marked with pain, love and forgiveness.

Tears began to spill down my flustered cheeks as the events that happened before play through my blurred vision. Voices echoed through the building as panic ran through my veins like lightning. The door opened cautiously, blinding me with light.

I woke up with the sweat pouring down my face. I turned to my right and picked up my phone off the cabinet, it was only three-thirty in the morning. My head fell back onto the pillow.

I lay awake for hours wondering about the memory that had planted itself in the walls of my mind.

The sunlight filtered in-between the curtains, the sound of the singing birds whistled through the silence of the early morning hours.

Climbing out of bed, I felt the cold floorboards against my feet. A gentle snore escaped the lips of my four-month-old baby, Charles.

Walking over to his cot, I studied the pictures that lay upon the unit a family, just the two of us. I smiled at the one picture where Charles was actually smiling, you can see the innocence shine in his ocean eyes.

I stood there just admiring the small child beneath my presence before deciding to make my way downstairs, to where my day will begin.

After pouring a cup of tea, I decided to sit in the same old wooden chair that was placed in front of a large window that provided a view of beauty. You could see the waves crashing into the sand and the deep greys of the clouds hovering above the deep unknown.

As I was watching the sunrise further into the heavens, a cry echoed down the stairs and to the kitchen, a sigh parted my lips and the silence of the views had passed.

I walked back upstairs, opening the bedroom door revealing a blue-eyed baby boy staring through the side of his cot with tears streaming down his rosy red cheeks.

I picked him up feeling him relax against my touch.

"I think someone's hungry."

His eyes fluttered shut as I made my way down the stairs towards the kitchen. Once I got to the kitchen, I grabbed the bottle that I had prepared in those many sleepless hours and carefully leant back his tiny body.

His eyes opened slightly, I slowly placed the top of the rubber bottle against his lips.

Once he began to drink happily, I sat back in the chair and cherished the moment of the views, silence and the peaceful memory we share every morning.

After I finished feeding Charles, I placed the new dirty bottle in the warm soapy liquid that filled the sink, then made my way to the front room.

I placed Charles in his Moses basket that sat in the corner of the room next to the armchair.

Picking up the television remote, I turned on the TV and began scrolling through films to watch.

I was about halfway through a film when there was a knock at the door; it was odd because I lived so far out and have no relatives, some friends but none that would make an effort to come all the way out to the coast.

I hesitated and stood standing in the hallway. They knocked again but this time slightly harder.

I opened the door slowly to reveal a man in a long black coat.

"Hello, can I help you?" I asked unsure of what to say or what response I will receive.

"Hello, Miss Smith?" he questioned.

"That's me, may I ask who you are?"

"Yes, I'm Inspector Brown, may I come in?"

"Yes," I said unsure whether or not to trust this man.

I took him into the kitchen in which he sat down at the dining table at the far end of the room. I offered him a drink which he declined.

"Why are you here, Mr Brown?" I asked leaning against the worktop.

"I'm here to discuss your friend Ethan." As he said those words, my whole world froze.

"I'm sorry, sir, but what about Ethan, he died about thirteen months ago?"

"That's why I'm here. We are investigating his death; his case is now undergoing as a murder investigation," he said as he pulled out a note pad from his coat pocket.

"OK, what can I do to help?"

"I would just like to ask you some questions about your relationship with Ethan?"

"Sure," I replied not knowing what I was supposed to say other than what I had already told the police thirteen months ago.

"What were you to Mr Davies?"

"Ethan and I, we were just friends, we had been best friends since we were born, our parents lived next door to each other."

"So, you knew him well. What was Mr Davies like?"

"He was an amazing person; he had a wild personality. He never failed to put a smile on anyone's face. He could walk into a room and it would be like the rays of sun spread from wall to wall."

"So, you spent a lot of time with Mr Davies?"

"Yes, every day, since we could walk and talk. We would see each other for at least two or more hours a day. Well, that was until he met Jessica. We would still see each other but it wouldn't be the same, but I guess you could say we both started growing up and going our separate ways."

"Would I be right in saying that the months previous to Mr Davies murder you weren't in contact?"

"No, I mean we didn't meet each other much because he was moving in with Jessica, but we would still call and text whenever we got the chance."

Just as the Inspector went to fire the next question, Charles cries could be heard bouncing off the walls.

"Excuse me, I will be back in a second." The Inspector just nodded in response.

I calmly walked across the hallway into the front room, where I could see Charles had pushed his blanket off his body whilst squirming round in his Moses basket. I picked him up whilst resting him on the top half of my body and proceeding my way back into the kitchen.

The Inspector looked up as Charles and I walked into the kitchen.

"Who's this little fella?" the inspector asked.

"This is Charles." I sat down next to the Inspector, who was admiring Charles' features.

"How old?"

"He has just turned four months old a few days ago," I said as I watched the inspector search for what he would ask me next.

"You must have been pregnant, whilst Ethan was still alive, did he know about Charles?" The air stopped in my throat; I could feel my chest tighten.

"Yes, I was and unfortunately I didn't have the chance to tell Ethan." I let out a nervous laugh.

"Who is the father, if you don't mind me asking?" He looked at me like he had just asked the question for the fun of it, it was like he already knew.

"I would rather not talk about it, it's a time that I would rather not remember."

"That's fine, thank you for answering the questions, Miss Smith. I will be in contact if that's all right?" he said as he got up from his chair.

"That's fine, anything you need to know, I'm always here." I followed the Inspector out of the kitchen back into the hallway. I watched him unlock the door and walk out, turning around and giving Charles a slight wave.

That was it, then the door shut and his car pulled off.

I stood in silence for a while, cradling Charles softly in my arms.

After what felt like hours, I finally got Charles down for his afternoon nap, that's when I decided to go to the backroom and reminisce on some old memories.

I walked in, the stacks of photo albums still laid neatly on the computer table.

I sat down in the middle of the room, grabbing a few of the photo albums before sighing heavily.

Turning the first page, a lump began to form in the back of my throat. Two baby scans laid next to each other. I read over scribbles next to the photographs. They read,' Ethan's first scan, Olive's first scan.'

Tears formed along the surface of my eyes. On the next page were Ethan's and my second scans, I still can't believe to this day that his mother and mine fell pregnant at the same time.

After flipping through the first few pages of memories, I came across the year I remembered the most. There was a picture of Ethan and I sat in the back of a car on our first road trip to Scotland, our heads resting on one another whilst we slept peacefully.

I looked at how happy we all were, my mum and his both single parents, who never let Ethan and me down.

As I got to the end of the photo album, my tears covered the years of pages, but they soon dried up when I came across the most recent picture, which Ethan had gotten me for Christmas one year.

It was a picture of Ethan, Jessica and I, I look as though I don't belong in the picture that was taken. I stood so far away from Ethan like I didn't even know who he was anymore. I never understood what he saw in her, after all, she wasn't innocent.

After sitting there in deep thought, I was interrupted by Charles, who was simply crying for his feed. As I walked out of the room, slowly shutting the door, I remembered why I never went in there. It was filled with so much love, desire and innocence.

I have a new life now, I looked up at the walls to see portraits of Charles and me. Smiling to myself, I quickly went to attend to Charles.

I stared into Charles' blue eyes and I couldn't help myself but see his father in him.

It got me thinking about what if everything was different, it was confusing how time could be so peaceful but then so painful.

Hours went by as I sat and watched TV, occasionally seeing to Charles's needs. I looked up at the clock to see that the time had flown by and it was now pitch-black outside. I took this as a time to rest.

I placed Charles on my shoulder and walked calmly up the stairs. Just before putting him down, he became unsettled, so I swayed my body side to side to prevent him from waking up completely.

Once I had put Charles to bed, I decided that it wouldn't hurt to have one more peek at the photo albums in the back room.

Sighing heavily, I pushed open the door and flicked the light on. I lifted the albums from the side shelf and placed them on the floor.

I opened the first page and saw a recent picture of Ethan and me standing next to my mum's hospital bed. I remember that day like the back of my hand, it was the day before she passed.

Flashback:

"Hey, Olive," my mum croaked.

"Hey, Mum, how are you doing?"

"As good as I can get. I see you have brought Ethan and his mother along today?"

"Of course, Mum, they wouldn't miss seeing you for the world, you know that!" Ethan and his mother walked over to the other side of the bed. Ethan's mum, Susan, sat at the end of my mum's bed and smiled at her before starting a conversation.

Ethan and I sat in chairs opposite each other, it had been weeks since we last saw one another because he had been seeing Jessica so much.

"Hi, Olive," he smiled weakly.

"Hi, Ethan." I looked down not wanting to make eye contact. "Sorry, I haven't seen you much lately, it's just Jess and I are really busy moving in together."

"It's fine, I understand it's a big step in life."

"It's not fine, I could have at least messaged you or even called you."

"Honestly, it's fine." I smiled at him to give him some reassurance.

Just as he went to reply, his mum called us both over.

"You two sit on the bed, we need a picture of you and this wonderful woman." She smiled at my mum and my mum let out a small but grateful laugh.

We sat at either side of my mum on the bed holding her hands and then Susan snapped the picture.

Not long after the picture was taken, Ethan had to rush off to help Jessica finish with moving in their new home.

I was then left to listen to the two women ramble on about their lives and how they can't believe their babies are twenty-one.

End of Flashback

I sat there taking in all the emotions of that day and the painful days that followed.

Our mothers were right; it was crazy how we both are twenty-one now, well, I'm soon to be twenty-two now.

The longer I sat there, the more I realised how much this world can change within seconds.

I looked over some more pictures before deciding that it was probably best that I headed off to bed because I know that Charles will surely be awake once or twice throughout the night.

I placed the albums back on the shelf, then exited the room and quietly made my way into bed. I laid there for a while before my eyes got heavy and I couldn't stay awake any longer.

The rain crashed against the bedroom window, a branch scraped the side of the windowpane and startled me awake.

I rested my back into the soft pillow, rolled over and tried to close my eyes, but that dream that haunts me every night keeps me awake. I wish I could know whose fragile body I'm holding, who's house I sit upon the floor in and who's blood-stained my skin.

Too many questions filled my brain, so I decided to get up and make myself a cup of tea.

I arrived at the kitchen and flipped the kettle switch on and waited for the cold water to boil but found myself zoning out all the time that I had missed the kettle click to tell me the water had boiled. Not bothered whether it was cold or hot, I poured it into the mug that sat on the counter.

I walked over to my favourite place in the house, the big window that shared so many views with me.

The sea was stormy, you could see the twists and the rolls of the ocean's waves, the deep blues were no longer, the water was a dark grey.

The moon managed to dodge the thunder clouds that strolled across the open night sky.

I stayed there just admiring the view for a few hours until my eyes became heavy again.

I walked sluggishly up the stairs and collapsed on the bed. My eyelids dropped and that was it, lights out.

I awoke to see the sun bursting through the cracks in the curtains. I turned to my left to face Charles' cot to see he wasn't crying but smiling at me through the bars.

I decided at that moment that we should go to town and make a day of our lives and not be stuck in this house for hours on end.

After two hours of getting myself and Charles ready, I parked my car next to the local supermarket and got Charles out the car.

I placed him in his pram that had barely been used and made my way towards the shops.

I entered a shop that I always used to come to when I was in town with Ethan.

Just as I went around the corner of an aisle, I heard a voice that I recognised.

"Olive?"

"Oh, gosh, hey, Tyler."

I remember now. Tyler was one of my best friends through school, we used to sit at the back of the maths class together.

"Olive, you have a child now, a lot has changed since I moved away?" She scrunched her eyebrows up in a knot.

"Yeah, I have a kid now, his name is Charles and it doesn't seem that long ago since you moved away."

"Yeah, I know it doesn't, but it was just under two years ago."

I nodded in agreement to what she said. "Olive, I'm sorry to hear about Ethan."

"It's all right, I guess."

"How are you holding up?"

I thought about telling her the truth about everything, but I couldn't do that now. What's done is done.

"Yeah, I'm holding up. Hey, Tyler, do you fancy coming to have lunch with Charles and me?".

"Yeah, sounds great, just let me pay for these."

I waited outside the store whilst Tyler paid for her items. It didn't take her long before she was stood outside the shop, her shopping bags roped around her slight arms.

"Here, you can put them on the pram if you want?" She nodded, placing them over the handlebars of the pram.

We made our way downtown having an occasional conversation, that's what I always loved about Tyler, that when we were together, we would speak, but if we landed in silence, it was never awkward, we just enjoyed each other's company.

It wasn't long until we came to the old cafe at the end of the town where we all used to come and hang out after school on Fridays and pretty much every weekend.

We walked through the door to the smell of fresh cakes and the aroma of coffee hitting us.

"Wow, this hasn't changed at all," Tyler said as she spotted a table in the far corner.

"Nope, it sure hasn't." I smiled at her.

We both picked up a menu and ordered our regular lunch meal.

Whilst we waited for the food to be served, I thought it would be a good idea to give Charles his feed. I gently took him out of his pram and laid him across my lap.

"So, who's the lucky fella?" Tyler asked. I gulped not wanting to say anything, I wanted to avoid the conversation.

"I don't really want to talk about him if that's OK with you. I would just rather not say anything about it." She gave me a questioning look, then shrugged her shoulders.

"Can I hold him?"

"Yeah, of course." I slowly handed Charles over to Tyler and watched her face in awe as she took in his features.

"His eyes are so blue, they are beautiful." Tyler expressed her first impressions of Charles with mostly' awe, look at his little dimples 'and 'his smile is so cute', this made me smile so much to see my old friend admiring a creation of my future.

Time flew by. After lunch, Tyler, Charles and I went around some more shops, which contained Tyler mostly buying things and talking about how she's moving back to Jackwood with her husband, yes, she got married a few months ago, nothing special just a small family wedding, no friends, just as she had planned her whole life.

It was coming up to 4 o'clock and I decided to get going. Charles was getting restless and it had been a long day in general.

As we walked to our cars, I gave Tyler my address and told her to visit anytime. Before we both got into our cars, we exchanged numbers so we could keep in contact.

It wasn't a long drive home.

Just as I pulled into the driveway, it began to rain. I quickly rushed out of the car, then picked up Charles and ran in through the front door.

Finally, in the warmth of my own home, I placed Charles on the sofa and plonked myself next to him. I watched him smiling at me.

"You are going to be so much like your father," and with saying that, I picked him up and placed him on my chest.

I could feel his small hands nestle their way between my chest and his body as he became comfortable.

After a few hours of watching TV, I started to get tired. I could feel my vision becoming blurry and the sound of the TV became muffled. I picked up Charles and wrapped him in his baby blue blanket, then took us both up to bed.

For the first time in weeks, I managed to sleep the whole night through and so did Charles. I woke up feeling refreshed. I grabbed my phone from the nightstand and the first thing I saw was Tyler had messaged me asking if she could come around at noon.

I messaged Tyler back letting her know that it was fine.

I sat on the edge of my bed and listened to the silence and watched the birds fly from tree to tree outside the window.

A whimper came from the cot beside me and I knew that Charles had woken up, so I walked over to his cot and picked him up, humming slightly to calm him down.

I lay Charles down on my bed surrounding his safety with pillows, whilst I got dressed.

I decided on wearing a pair of blue jeans with a white sweatshirt. I glanced at myself in the mirror and smiled at my reflection finally becoming happy again.

I went over to a small set of draws and pulled out a small pair of baby jeans and a navy jumper that never fails to bring out his precious blue eyes.

I placed the clothing over his tiny body and stared at him in disbelief, how could I create such a beautiful human?

I placed Charles on his play mat in the middle of the front room whilst I went around the house tidying every inch of every room before Tyler arrived.

After tidying, I went back to the front room and lay across the sofa watching Charles play with the toys that dangled above his head.

It was not long past noon that there was knock at the door. I rushed off the sofa to answer the door, excited to have a company.

I opened the door to be greeted by a smiley Tyler, who had bought flowers and a card, I looked at her with a confused expression.

"There for you as a congratulation at becoming a mum. I know it's late, but I couldn't not get you anything." She smiled handing me the flowers and the card before walking through the door.

"This is such a beautiful home," she said as she ran her fingers over the pictures of Charles and I that hung proudly on the wall.

I took her into the front room where Charles now laid fast asleep on his play mat.

"He's adorable," she beamed as she sat down on the sofa. I just nodded in response.

"Would you like tea or coffee?" I asked remembering what my mum taught me about having company around.

"Yeah, I will have a tea, please." As soon as she said that I disappeared into the kitchen.

I was waiting for the kettle to boil when I heard a sweet laugh echoing through the house. I walked out of the kitchen and placed my ear against the door of the front room.

"You look just like your daddy, I don't know why your mum won't admit it, he'd be proud of you."

Hearing those words made my heart flutter, but that didn't last long as the memories flooded back making my heart drop.

I went back to the kitchen, poured the cups of tea, then walked back across to the front room making sure to hide behind a smile.

"Here you go." I handed Tyler her tea.

"So, what's it like living alone?" Tyler questioned.

"It's nice, I guess sometimes it can be hard with Charles and even lonely," I admitted, Tyler just nodded and took a sip of her tea.

"Would you like to watch a film, like old times?" I asked, looking over to where she was sat.

"Yeah, that would be nice." I grabbed the remote and flicked through the channels. It took us ages to agree on a film, but when we both finally agreed on one, we both turned to each other and laughed, this was so much like the old days.

Halfway through the film, Charles started to cry and I just sighed. Tyler must have noticed because she picked him up and started to feed him his bottle, Tyler definitely saw that I was struggling all alone, on my own.

After about twenty minutes, Charles finally settled again and Tyler sat him in the middle of us on the sofa.

About an hour later, the film finished, Tyler looked at me and I looked at her, both of us thinking what could we do now.

"What would you say if I asked you if you want to walk along the beach, it's beautiful?" I added. I knew Tyler was never a fan of the beach because she hated sand, it got everywhere.

"Yeah, sure, that would be nice, we could do with getting some fresh air, especially you, Olive because I know you hardly go anywhere." She got up and picked Charles up from the sofa, and smiled at her own comment before walking out past me into the hallway.

Whilst Tyler got herself and Charles ready, I got some shoes on and ran out to the car to grab Charles' pram out of the boot.

Finally, as I just set the pram up, Tyler came out with Charles in her arms all wrapped up in his little grey jacket and his blanket.

She came over and sat him in his pram and then we started walking towards the beach.

We walked for a few minutes before the sand hit the bottoms of our shoes. The grey sky had held back the rain and you could see a breakthrough of blue sky coming through the clouds.

"This is so pretty like you wake up to this every day and it never stays the same, a different view for every day. You're lucky, Olive." Tyler stopped and took in her surroundings.

"Yeah, I know," was all I could say because she was right, this view never failed to amaze me, every day it was different.

We walked right to the edge of the beach before the cliffs and rocks prevented us from going any further. It was so nice to just have random conversations with Tyler and catch up on the moments we both missed.

The sun had just come out to disappear as the night sky rolls in.

"Wow, this sunset is magical, looks at those deep pinks creating its shadow across the ocean waves," Tyler said as she stopped in her tracks to take in the beautiful encounter.

It was so elegant, the way the deep pinks mixed with the reds and different shades of colours, the sky looked like a huge strawberry milkshake.

We stood there for another five minutes before we finally started to head back up to the house.

When I got to the front door, I didn't know whether or not Tyler wanted to stay for dinner or if she had had enough of me.

"Hey, Tyler, do you want to stay for dinner?"

"Yeah, I would love to, I don't want to intrude though."

"Don't be silly, come on, let's get inside where it's warm and I will make us some food."

"I can feed Charles whilst you make the dinner?"

"That would be great if you could do that. Thank you, Tyler."

I hugged her slim frame and walked into the house with Charles. I slid his pram to the side and motioned for Tyler to pick him up and take him into the front room for his feed.

As soon as Tyler settled down with Charles, I rushed into the kitchen, excited to be hosting a dinner, even if it was just for the two of us, it was more than enough.

An hour later, I called Tyler into the kitchen. I gave it a few minutes until she walked in. She looked over at the table, which was glowing with food. Tyler just stood there stunned.

"Wow, Olive, this is amazing."

"It's nothing, honestly."

I sat down across from Tyler and watched as she scooped a selection of food onto her plate.

"Did Charles go down OK?"

"Out like a light," she said, her face stuffed full of food.

We spent the rest of our dinner silent and ramming our faces full of delicious food. It was so nice to eat with someone.

About an hour later, we were sat at the table laughing over some old memories from our school years.

"Do you remember when you asked that Tom guy out and he turned to you and said you're really pretty but I'm gay and I'm not turning straight for you?" Tyler and I laughed in unison. I remember that it was such a great day.

"Yeah, do you remember Tyler, when we went to that cafe and your crush was in there and you stuttered so bad? The guy turned to you and said,' Has a cat got your tongue?', that was funny." I laughed so hard when I said that and Tyler's face went a bright shade of red.

"Hey, I've got an idea. Do you want to see some old photos of us from school?" I asked regretting it as soon as I opened my mouth, I really didn't want to go back into that room, let alone Tyler finding all the pictures of Ethan and me.

"Yes, this is going to be so fun," she squealed as she put her empty dish in the sink.

I followed her out into the hallway and pointed to the stairs and indicated for her to lead the way whilst I got Charles from the living room.

I lay Charles in his cot and then went to meet Tyler in the back room, which was located right at the far end of the house.

I walked in to see she had already started wandering through the photo albums. As I got closer, I could see which one she was holding and I hoped she hadn't gotten that far through it.

"Is this what Ethan got you for Christmas?" I just nodded and sat on the floor next to her.

"I didn't know you guys practically grew up alongside each other and have known one another since birth."

She asked in disbelief.

"Yeah, we didn't tell anyone, I don't know why, but Ethan wanted to keep it a secret."

"What, why would he want to do that? This is amazing. You guys had such a good bond."

"Had a good bond." I lowered my head in the realisation that he would never be coming back.

Once the awkward silence had evaporated in the air, I grabbed a second album. My mum always took photos and placed them in albums, she said it was like a secret keep safe to re-live memories.

I lifted this light blue album, which read across the front, 'Olive's years of school', then I handed it to Tyler and smiled.

She opened the album to see she was the first person to be seen when someone was to open this album.

She stood next to me after our first week of school, she was the first person and mainly the only person I ever made friends with.

She had her arm over my right shoulder, we both looked super young. To see her smiling at the picture brought a smile to my face and I knew she was thinking back to that day, just like I was.

We spent the last two hours looking over the old pictures and laughing. It felt so good to be reminded of the past and to be happy with the outcome.

Time flew by and we both became tired, so Tyler made the first move by getting up off the floor.

"Well, what a day this has been, but time's ticking now, I should probably get going," Tyler suggested.

"Yeah, that's fine. I guess I will see you again sometime." I walked Tyler out of the back room, took one last glance at the room, then switched the light off and followed her to the front door.

"I will see you again soon." She turned around to face me.

"Of course, wouldn't miss seeing you again for the world," I smiled widely at her as she opened the front door.

I watched as she walked out into the cold of the night and then got in her car. Then before I knew it, I was waving as she drove off into the distance.

I made my way back into the house, shut the door and smiled to myself, it was one of the best days I'd had in such a long time.

The next day, I woke up, got Charles dressed and fed. Then we headed back to town, it was now or never to change our lives around, no more being stuck inside the house.

After an hour of getting everything ready, Charles and I were buckled into the car. Then I started the car and drove off towards town.

We arrived in town about midday, which was nice because the streets were filled with different faces with every moment that passed.

I got Charles out of the back of the car and put him in his pram, then we set off towards the shops. I wanted to find a photo album that would be great for Charles to start placing pictures in from the day he was born up to now and every magical moment after.

I entered a shop and went straight to the back, I knew there were photo albums by here somewhere because this is where my mum used to get mine from.

On the top shelf, I spotted a pale blue and white large photo album that read across the front,' To make a memory, you first have to be one'. It was perfect.

I grabbed it from the shelf, satisfied that I'd found the perfect one.

As I turned the corner to reach the cashier, I bumped into someone, someone whom I'd never thought I would see again. Ethan's mum.

"Olive, hi, oh gosh, how are you? How have you been?" she questioned.

"Susan, yeah, I'm good, thank you, what about yourself?"

"I'm great, I thought I would come back to my home town and visit some old friends."

Susan left after Ethan passed away, she said there was too much negativity around here with my mum passing, then a few weeks later her sons.

"That's nice, do you plan on doing much else whilst you're down?"

"Yeah, don't tell anyone, but the real reason I'm here isn't really to visit friends. I was contacted by an Inspector a few weeks ago, he told me he had a lead in Ethan's case and that I needed to be around just in case of any needed information." I gulped, I could feel the nerves rushing through my body.

"That's great news, Susan. I really hope they do him justice, after all, that's what he deserves," I said, just barely audible.

"Who's this little fella? I didn't know you had a son, Olive? You should have told me, I would have come to visit." As soon as she said that, I froze.

"Olive?" Susan waved her hand in front of my face bringing me back to reality.

"Oh, right, so this is Charles and if I'm honest, I kept it quiet. I had problems with the father, which I have vowed not to talk about. I'm sorry if that sounds rude, but it's how I deal with it." I said, rushing out the last sentence, sucking in a breath of air.

"He looks like Ethan, don't you think?" As soon as those words slipped her lips, my heart shattered into a million pieces.

"He does. Ethan always said if he died before me, he'd find a way to remind me of him every day".

"Well, he did a fine job." She smiled holding on to Charles' tiny hands.

"I take it you have your own place?"

"Yeah, I do. I've got a house outside of town, right next to the beach."

"I will come to visit one day whilst I'm here, just send me your address, I've still got the same number."

"That would be nice, Susan."

"Right, I will let you get back to your shopping because that album isn't going to fill itself. You're so like your mother." She smiled and gave me a small wave as she walked out of the shop.

That was something I never thought I'd have to do, I never thought I'd have that conversation in my life, but I guess I can't avoid it.

I continued my way to the counter, where I handed the lady the photo album.

"I take it this album is for this little man?" The woman who was serving said, leaning over the counter and pointing at Charles.

"Yeah, it is."

"Well, have a nice day." She smiled, handing me the photo album.

It felt weird to speak to so many people in one day. I used to speak to everyone in town but ever since that day, I just never left the house.

The day flew by and Charles was starting to get unsettled. It was more than likely because he was hungry and to be honest, I could hear my stomach grumble every now and then.

We made our way back to the same cafe that I was sat in with Tyler the other day. I walked through the door sitting at the same table right at the back in a corner, just a simple little booth.

I noticed that it wasn't busy today, it was very quiet. I could hear some muffled voices coming from behind me and it took me a few seconds but I recognised the voices. It was Tyler and Susan, but wait, why are they together. I didn't even know they knew each other.

I tried not to overthink it, but then my mind got the better of me and I put two and two together. I remembered Susan say she was called to town by the Inspector, what if Tyler had too.

"He definitely looks like Ethan." I could hear Tyler saying to Susan.

"Yeah, but she would have told us if there was something going on, I've known that girl since the day she was born," Susan stated.

I told myself to stop listening because it would just make me paranoid, but I couldn't help myself.

"I don't know, she doesn't really seem herself and Charles definitely looks like Ethan."

That's the last thing I heard before Charles started crying for his feed, then I heard nothing but silence come from behind me.

As I was giving him his feed, I heard footsteps coming towards the table. I think it was fair to say I panicked.

"Olive?" It was Tyler.

"Hey, Tyler," was all I managed to say.

"What are you doing here?" she asked.

"Thought I'd take Charles out for the day instead of being stuck inside."

"Oh, OK. Well, this isn't awkward." Tyler knew I had heard her conversation with Susan.

"I'm sorry about what I said earlier, it was nothing bad, I swear. It's just Charles does look so much like Ethan. Olive why don't you just admit it?" Her sad eyes were now connecting with mine.

I could feel myself start to cry, I let one tear fall and then the rest just came running down my cheeks after.

"I don't want to talk about it," I choked out.

I placed Charles back in his pram, gathered my stuff and walked out of the cafe leaving Tyler stood still in utter shock. I could hear her calling my name, but I kept facing forward and carried on walking away.

I made my way straight back to the car not daring to look back. When I got to the car, I put Charles in his seat, then flung the pram in the boot.

I jumped in the driver's side, slammed the door shut. I wanted to scream out loud, but it would unsettle Charles, so I just silently cried, resting my forehead on the steering wheel. I sat there and cried for a few minutes before pulling myself together. I then started the engine and made my way back home.

It wasn't long before I pulled up outside the house. Then with all the effort I had left, I got myself out of the car.

Making my way round to get Charles out of the car, I clocked my reflection in the car window and thought to myself, how pathetic I had become.

I got Charles out of the car and inside the house, where I lay spread across the sofa with him on my chest. I grabbed the TV remote and switched on the TV, putting on a random programme.

Before I knew it, we were both asleep.

I woke up, the TV had turned itself off and the room had become pitch black. Looking out of the window, I could faintly see the moonlight glistening on the bushes.

Slowly pushing myself up and gently moving Charles, I stood up and made my way into the hallway.

As I turned to walk up the stairs, I noticed a white envelope hanging from the letterbox. Ignoring it, I proceeded to put Charles to bed.

Once I had placed Charles in his cot, I then climbed into my own. I just lay there trying to get to sleep, but curiosity got the better of me. I had to know what was in that envelope.

I got out of bed and went straight for the envelope. Once I had it in my hands, I recognised the handwriting straight away. The front of the envelope read, 'To my one and only Olive'.

I opened the envelope to reveal the messy handwritten letter.

'I hope this letter reaches you in time. I received your note that was stuck to the back of my wardrobe door. I'm so sorry that I couldn't be there for your first scan, or should I say our first scan. It's been so hard and I'm sorry that I got you into this mess. We grew up together and I know this is not how we saw our lives going and part of me would turn back the clocks to make it all right again. It kills me to have to say this but I'm going to keep it short and sweet. I can't be a part of your life anymore; we have taken different paths that don't match. Before you say how did I know you were pregnant and that I missed our first scan, it was because I was at the hospital with Jessica. We lost our child today, she had a miscarriage. I saw you were there and overheard you talking to a nurse and I knew that blue-eyed boy you spoke about was me. So, here it goes, Olive Smith, I will regret this forever, even afterlife, but I need to move on with Jessica, I don't need the stress, I love her and I'm sorry, Olive.

From your one and only Ethan'

My world just crumbled from under my feet, my head spun around. Everything felt like it was unfolding in front of me.

This is what I needed to hear to move on. I needed to be kicked down before I could build myself up, slowly but surely.

Chapter Two
The Lifeline Unfolds

The weekend came round fast, the days just flew by.

I hadn't been out of the house in days and decided that it was enough, I'm going to pull myself together and make a life for Charles and me.

I took Charles into town to do the food shop. I planned on having a picnic on the beach as it was such a beautiful day, the sun was blazing down, but you could still feel the cold air nipping at your heels.

Making our way to the supermarket, I spotted Tyler. She looked right at me with an apologetic expression plastered across her face. I just turned my head the other way and continued with my day. I felt horrible, but this was how I dealt with things, everyone is different.

I arrived at a shop. I was paranoid; I felt like all eyes were on me. As I walked through the aisles, my world began to slow down and the room began to spin around me. The next thing I know is that everything went black, all I could hear was silence.

Slowly opening my eyes, a light shone brightly. I tried to focus my vision but everything was blurred. Panic waves flooded over my body. Where am I? Where is Charles?

After about ten minutes, my eyes began to adjust and I could see wires attached to my body. I could see someone sleeping in the chair beside me and I could see Charles sound asleep in his pram.

I watched out the door as nurses and doctors attended to others. I watched them concentrate hard on the paperwork that they held so strongly in their hands like they held life in their palms.

Careful not to wake Tyler and Charles up, I reached over to the table to grab a glass of water.

As I was moving towards the table, I accidentally nudged Tyler's foot. It didn't take much to wake Tyler up.

"Olive, you're awake? I need to inform a nurse." She rushed to her feet, not giving me time to ask her what happened. She was gone.

Confused, I tugged at the wires, which were pierced into my skin. It sent pain through my body, I cried out in a struggle, becoming uneasy in the situation.

The next thing I knew was two strong hands grabbed my shoulders and pushed me back into the bed. I couldn't understand what they were saying, their voices were muffled.

"Calm down, Olive, you might hurt yourself. Just relax."

I looked above me to see a doctor. She stared at me, giving me a reassuring smile.

"Olive, my name is Doctor James. You were brought in by ambulance, we aren't sure as to why you collapsed, but to make things easier for us, we are going to need to ask you some questions that are concerning some tests we took whilst you were asleep."

"OK," I said, not wanting to make eye contact with anyone, I felt like a disappointment.

"OK, Olive, when was the last time you had food?"

"I…Um…"

"We need you to be truthful with us now, Olive. Remember some of these are just general questions we have to ask everyone, do you feel comfortable with your friend being in the room?"

"Yes, she can stay."

"So, Olive, when was the last time you ate?"

"About four days ago."

"So, you haven't eaten anything at all in the last four days?"

"I've had a few biscuits, but I haven't eaten enough, I know I haven't."

"OK. Do you struggle living home alone with a newborn? I understand if you do."

"No, no, I can cope absolutely fine, I've just had a lot on my mind."

"Have you had much sleep?"

"I would say I get two or more hours at night if I'm lucky."

"Right, just a few more questions, then we will be done," she said as I watched her pen write frantically in her note pad.

The doctor asked me a few more questions, then she said she would be back to let me know about the test results, which left me to ask Tyler what happened.

"Tyler what…what happened?"

"Well, all I saw was you placing food in a basket, then out of nowhere you just dropped."

"I don't remember picking any food up, I remember going down the right aisle."

"After you fell to the ground, I ran over to you. Your body looked lifeless, Olive, you looked so pale, it scared me."

"I'm sorry, Tyler. I never meant for any of this to happen and I'm sorry I've been ignoring you." I bowed my head down at how childish my actions have been.

"Olive, don't you dare be sorry about any of this, this is not your fault. Everyone reacts in different ways and I'm sorry, I should have never have spoken about you behind your back."

Tyler walked over to the side of the bed and just sat there hugging me. We sat there and just cried in each other's company.

Pulling away from Tyler's embrace, I saw a little head moving around from the side of the pram. I tapped on Tyler's shoulder and pointed towards the pram, then mouthed one, two, three.

Right on cue, Charles started crying, Tyler turned to face me and started giggling.

I sat upright against the soft bed that was now folded all the way up. Tyler took Charles from his pram and passed him across to me.

"Hey, little man." I stroked him and smiled down at him.

It was about two hours later that the doctor came back.

"Right, everything looks normal, just your blood sugars were a tad too low for my liking. That is what caused you to pass out. So, Miss Smith, I would like you to eat a little more than just a biscuit because I think you've learned that a biscuit a day does not keep the doctor away." She sniggered at her own comment.

Once she left the room, a nurse entered and kindly took all the wires off my body and then I was free to go.

We reached the entrance of the hospital and Tyler and I were about to go our separate ways when I realised my car was still in town.

"Tyler, my cars not here! Would you mind taking me to collect it from town, it's kind of a walk otherwise?"

"Yeah, sure." She laughed.

"Wait, you don't have a seat for Charles?"

"Of course, I do. How do you think I got him here, you went alone in the ambulance? I was going to ask you to come back to my car, I thought you were following me."

She laughed even harder. How could I be so stupid?

We walked over to her car, she put Charles in his car seat. Then I put the pram in the boot.

Once we were all in the car, we set off back towards town so I could get my car.

It didn't take long to reach the car park, where my car was parked. I reached the door handle to get out of Tyler's car, but before I could wrap my hand round it, she grabbed my wrist.

"Now, Olive, if you ever need me, please call me or text me. Just let me know. I'm here for you. If you want to talk, I will wait for you, just talk to me when you're ready."

"I will, Tyler, I'm just learning to stand," I whispered the last bit, before climbing out of the car and making my way round to get Charles. I picked him up before making my way to the boot, then I realised I had done this all back to front.

"Tyler? Can you help me get the pram out of the boot?"

It took her seconds before she got out of the car, opened the boot and placed the pram on the floor. She opened it up like she had done this a million times before.

I just sent her a questioning look, she just stared back at me blankly.

"Tyler, do you want to come for a picnic tomorrow? I was going to have one today but things took a different turn." I giggled at her to which she just nodded in response, not really making eye contact. It was like she was hiding something. I just thought best to let it go, it had been such a long day.

I got back into my car, double-checking that Charles was strapped in securely before giving Tyler a small wave and driving off.

As I was driving home, I wondered why Tyler had acted so weirdly after I cracked that joke about her putting up the pram. Did Tyler have a child? How could she hide something like that from me?

It wasn't long before Charles and I arrived home. I couldn't wait to put Charles to bed and climb into bed myself. It had been such an eventful day.

As soon as I got inside, I rushed to the kitchen, quickly made Charles' bottles, then made my way upstairs.

I lay Charles in his cot and fed him his bottle. It didn't take long before his eyelids shut, then he was out like a light.

I turned around and looked over at the comforting bed that called my name. I quickly changed into a baggy top and some shorts. Then I slithered my way underneath the covers, resting my head back on the cloud-like pillows. I sighed heavily before letting the darkness surround my vision. My eyes closed and I gently drifted off to sleep.

The rays of the morning sun lay across the end of the white sheets bringing light to a dark room.

Looking over to the bedside table, I saw the time and jumped out of bed. It wouldn't be long until Tyler would be here.

I decided to message her to let her know I was only just getting up and then I would proceed to dress Charles and prepare the food. Tyler must have been waiting for me to message her as I instantly received a message back.

Walking over to Charles' cot, I decided to throw some old clothes on today as we would be down the beach.

I picked Charles out of his cot, then laid him on the unmade bed. I dressed him in a pair of black tracksuit bottoms and a plain blue sweatshirt. For myself, I decided on wearing a baggy pair of blue jeans and a black sweatshirt.

An hour flew by, then Tyler turned up, wearing roughly the same type of old clothing that Charles and I were dressed in.

Tyler let herself in whilst I packed the last of the food into the cooler bag. I heard laughter coming from the living room, which indicated that Tyler had found Charles and was more than likely suffocating him with hugs.

Once everything was ready, I grabbed the pram from the car; whilst Tyler walked out the front door holding Charles ready to place his tiny body in the seat.

After a couple of minutes, we were all set to head off to the beach. The weather wasn't too bad, slightly cloudy with a cool breeze weaving its way through the strands of my hair.

We walked about halfway across the sand lit beach before we stopped and decided that this was far enough, we would just have our picnic here.

"So, how are you feeling?" Tyler said, breaking the silence. I thought about it for a few seconds before deciding on giving her a truthful answer.

"I guess not so good."

"Are you struggling with Charles? Because if you are, I could come live with you and help—" Before she could finish her sentence, I cut her off.

"It's not that, Tyler, I'm not struggling with Charles. I'm struggling to come to terms with everything."

"With what?" I froze, I just couldn't tell her, well, at least not yet. It turns out this was going to be harder than I thought.

"Never mind. I thought I was ready to talk but I'm not." I shook my head in shame.

"That's OK, everything takes time. I'm always here for you, you know." She placed her hand on top of mine and gave me a wide smile.

Time flew by quickly, the majority of the time we spent laughing at old memories or laughing at Charles as he sat, his bare hands and feet covered in sand.

We came to an agreement to stay there for another hour because we loved the silence of the beach and Charles was still enjoying himself.

Looking back at the house, I realised how lucky I was to be so far yet so close to everyone and everything. I see these beautiful views that change almost every day, but part of me couldn't feel completely whole after what happened, there will always be that emptiness feeling trapped in my chest.

"Are you ready?" Tyler said, standing up and brushing the remaining sand off her joggers.

"Yes." I smiled as I got up and repeated her actions.

Tyler packed everything away whilst I tried my best to clean the sand off Charles. I knew I was going to have to bath him after this because he was covered from head to toe.

Just as we came to the end of the beach, I stopped and faced Tyler unsure of whether or not I should ask this.

"Hey, Tyler, do you want to stay the night? I've got spare clothes and a toothbrush in the spare bedroom." I looked up at her to see her in deep thought as if she was debating on what she wanted to do.

"Yeah, sure, I mean I don't see why not, it will be fun and nice for you to have some company." She smiled back.

We finally reached the front door, just as the air became colder. Tyler pushed the pram through the door and into the hallway before taking Charles out of it and making her way into the living room and placing him down on his play mat.

I headed to the kitchen to boil the kettle for Charles' night feed and a cup of tea for Tyler and me.

Almost five minutes had passed before I realised that I had yet again been staring into thin air and that the kettle had already boiled.

Tyler stood in the entrance of the kitchen, she just stared at me with a concerned look on her face.

"This happens often, I will just blackout for a few minutes, I just don't understand why it happens."

I pushed the feeling of wanting to cry away, then continued with pouring the cups of tea and Charles' night feed.

"Olive, are you OK?" I could feel her presence.

"Yes, I think so?" I questioned my own emotional feelings.

"You know I'm here if you ever want to talk and before you say anything back to that, I know you aren't ready to talk yet. I just want you to know that you are never alone." As I listened to the words that parted her lips, I felt her hand rest upon my shoulder.

After Tyler removed her hand, she left the kitchen. Tyler realised that I wasn't in the mood to talk about the situation.

I just put a smile on my face and made the teas. Then I placed the pre-made bottles on the side of the counter, then grabbed the teas.

Finally, I made my way to the living room to be treated by such a peaceful sight. Charles was fast asleep, his tiny body spread across the middle of the sofa.

Gently, I sat next to the innocent child and handed Tyler her cup. We sat in silence for a while just taking in the memories we shared on the beach and the events that occurred from the previous days.

"What do you want to watch?" I motioned to Tyler whilst picking up the remote.

"How about we watch a crime and investigation programme?"

"Yes, that's fine." I remember how Tyler and I used to watch these kinds of programmes all the time.

It got to about midnight and I could feel myself becoming tired and I knew Tyler was too because every now and then, you could hear a yawn escape her lips.

"I think it's time to head off to bed, I will show you where your room is." I got up taking Charles with me, moving him swiftly in my arms.

Tyler followed me out of the living room and up the stairs. Before showing Tyler her room, I made a quick stop to place Charles in his cot, closing the bedroom door slowly behind me, being careful not to wake the sleeping child. I then motioned for Tyler to follow me. I lead her across the landing to a small set of stairs.

"This is your stop. If you need anything, you know where I am." I opened the door and switched the light on before turning on my heels and heading back to my room.

"Night, Olive." I heard Tyler whisper as she shut the door behind her.

"Night, Tyler," I whispered to myself as I walked into my own room and collapsed on the bed.

I jumped into bed in the clothes I was wearing, feeling too lazy and tired to be bothered to change into some pyjamas.

I let my body sink into the comfort of the bed and drifted off to sleep peacefully.

My breathing hitched, I felt sweat dripping down my head. I couldn't wake up, I began to panic.

A door opened, a shadow walked in frantically. I was dreaming. A man fell into my arms, I felt emotionally attached to him, but I couldn't make out who it was, my vision was blurry.

I looked over to where the window was to see the moonlight streaming through the curtains. Turning away from the window, I stopped still to see my reflection in the mirror. My whole body froze, I didn't dare to look down, all the memories from that night started flooding back.

My hands began to shake, my breathing was becoming shaky. I looked down to see his face, the one who had haunted my dreams for hours on end.

Blood trickled down the side of his head and onto my innocent skin. His facial expression changed from hurt too relaxed within seconds. His eyes shut and the world slowed down around me.

Sirens bellowed throughout the house, the sound bouncing off walls and echoing in my ears. The blue and red lights glistened through the windows lighting up the walls.

The door opened to reveal a heartbroken woman, whom I recognised, wait that's Jessica! The beating of my heart stopped as we made eye contact.

"What have you done?" she repeated screaming at me as officers held her back from the scene that lay in front of them.

The words stuck in my throat, I can't process anything, nothing makes sense. I felt numb, but I also felt a feeling that I've never felt before, but I couldn't describe it. I know I just needed to let go.

"I didn't do it," I yelled, my own voice now echoing through my mind. The officers started walking towards me and I just let his body drop, the pace of my heart quickened, I kept shouting I didn't do it.

I woke up, tears flooding my vision, I could hear Charles crying. Seconds later, Tyler ran into my room, her facial expression full of worry, she picked Charles up then looked directly at me.

"Olive, are you OK? What's going on?"

"I had a dream, the same dream that's been haunting me for months."

"What was the dream about?"

"I can't say." I mentally slapped myself because I needed to talk to someone, I needed to let go.

"Look to take some weight off your shoulders, why don't I have Charles for the rest of the night?"

I just nodded in response and watched Tyler walk out of my room cradling Charles, I laid back and tried to relax. I tried to let my mind drift off, but nothing was working, so I went downstairs. I walked down the stairs being careful not to make any noise.

Opening the kitchen door, I found myself walking towards the usual spot where I would sit when I couldn't sleep.

Pulling the chair out from underneath the table, I began to stare out of the window.

I was now in deep thought when I began thinking back to the dream that haunts me. This time, the dream was different. I felt things, emotions, feelings and his soft touch.

I was much more involved in this dream, a lot more happened, maybe I was starting to remember what happened that night. As much as I had taught myself to forget, maybe there was a reason I needed to remember. I was so deep in thought that I didn't even realise Tyler had come downstairs for Charles' night feed.

"How long have you been standing there?" I questioned.

"Long enough to know you're hiding something from me," she fired back. I let out a heavy sigh.

"Go tend to Charles, then come back and I shall attempt to tell you what's going on." Tyler grabbed his bottle and ran upstairs.

Whilst Tyler was gone, it felt like ages and my palms were starting to sweat.

Tyler came back downstairs roughly twenty minutes later. She pulled out the chair next to me and placed her hand on my knee.

"Right, Olive, tell me what's going on inside that head of yours?"

"OK, here we go. So, I've been having these dreams and it was only this evening that I realised what the dream was. I think deep down, I have known all along, but I never wanted to admit it."

"OK, what's the dream about?"

"I'm in a room, it's silent and I'm sat on my own peacefully until a male figure comes in collapsing into my arms. His face was stained with blood."

"Carry on."

"My vision is blurred, but it starts to clear when I see my own reflection in the mirror."

"Do you feel anything?"

"I felt a lot of things, I could feel his skin upon mine and I can feel my emotions."

"OK, is there anymore?"

"Yes, after I saw my own reflection in the mirror, I felt like I was going to be sick and for some reason, I couldn't get myself to look down. It was like I was frozen."

"OK." I could see Tyler was unsure of what to think about my dream.

"When I finally looked down, I could see the male laying across my lap. I could see his eyes closing, his facial expression went from hurt too relaxed. I watched his body become chilled like his soul left his body."

Tyler just sat there with a blank expression on her face. I wasn't sure whether I should carry on, I didn't want to but I knew I needed to.

"I couldn't make out who it was because of the blood covering his face and my vision close up was blurred by tears that spilled down my face."

"Olive, how long have you been having this dream?"

"A while."

"You need to talk to someone about this, Olive. I'm glad that you have told me, but you need someone who can help you. Is there any more to this dream or is that it?" She looked extremely concerned.

"I know, I just didn't think it would come to this stage. It's just a stupid dream, Tyler and yes, there is more, but the next part confuses me."

"OK, I'm listening."

"The door opens to reveal a woman, who's followed by some police officers. As my vision starts to become clear, I recognised the woman."

"Olive, who is the person?."

"It's um…I don't want to say, I can't."

"Olive, you can you have told me this much, so you can tell me who it is."

"It was Jessica."

"Wait, Jessica as in Ethan's Jessica?"

"Yes."

"Right, OK, this is interesting, did anything happen after she walked in?"

"Yes, she walked in and started screaming at me saying 'what have you done', she kept repeating it. I remember the pace of my heart quickened."

"What does she mean by what have you done?"

"I don't know, but she kept screaming it at me. Then the officers were holding her back. Once they had pushed her out of the room, they came towards me. I dropped the body of the male, then that's when I woke up."

"Olive, you really need to talk to someone about this and you are certain you don't know whose body you are holding?" Tyler looked at me, guilt spread right across her face.

46

"No."

"Olive, do you remember the night that Ethan died?"

"Yes, I was on my way to his house, but when I got there no one answered the door. Then the next thing I know is I was in the back of the ambulance having blood cleaned off my hands."

"Olive, don't you see?"

"See what, Tyler?"

"You were the person who held Ethan whilst he died; you were the last person he ever saw." I just sat there shocked, but why couldn't I remember it.

"Why can't I remember, Tyler?"

"Olive, the brain does funny things, it will black out the things that you don't want to remember. It's like a traumatic effect." In a way, this was all making sense.

"An inspector came to my house a few weeks ago, he was asking about you, Olive. He mentioned there was a girl inside the house holding Ethan's body but it wasn't Jessica and now I know it was you. You're the missing piece to Ethan's justice," she beamed like it was a good thing.

"Tyler, what if they think it was me who killed Ethan? What if I did?" Silence filled the air as the questions surround our minds.

Minutes passed and neither one of us said a word, we just sat in complete silence.

"Tyler, I'm going to bed. We can sort things out in the morning." Tyler didn't hesitate to agree with me. She stood up, hugged me tightly, then made her way back to bed.

I waited a few minutes waiting to hear Tyler shut her bedroom door.

Once I knew Tyler had gone to bed, I finally made my way back upstairs, but instead of going straight to bed, I made a quick detour.

Standing on the landing, I looked at the room, where a week ago Tyler and I laughed at the old memories that we shared. I opened the door slowly making sure to close it again before turning the light on.

I took a seat on the floor. I hadn't looked at this photo album since Ethan had died.

Opening the album, it revealed the first page. I closed my eyes. As I opened them again, I saw a picture of Ethan kissing my stomach with Charles' second scan in his right hand. I smiled at the memory until I remembered the events that took place just minutes after.

Flashback

I pulled up to Ethan's driveway. I'm finally going to tell him that I'm pregnant.

I got out of the car and knocked on the door, waiting patiently for him to answer.

"Hey Olive, just got your message. You got here fast, is everything OK?"

"Hi, I guess you could say it's kind of OK."

"OK, come in and tell me."

I followed him into his front room before taking a seat on his sofa.

"So, what's the news, Olive?"

"It's a lot to take in, I'm pregnant." Ethan stood still, trying to process what I just said.

"That's amazing, Olive," he said hesitantly.

"Yeah, I guess it is."

"Who's the lucky man?" Ethan wiggled his eyebrows and took a seat next to me.

"That's why I'm here. Ethan, you're the father." His face lit up like the morning sun.

"Wait, you can't be serious? Olive, that's amazing. I'm going to be a dad." He lifted the hem of my shirt.

"Olive, take a picture, then send it to me."

"Wait, have this too." I handed Ethan Charles' second scan.

He grabbed the scan from me, holding it tightly in his grip. As he kissed my stomach, I snapped the picture, but then within seconds everything changed.

Ethan stood up, threw the picture at me and started pacing around the room.

"It's not mine," he yelled, causing me to flinch.

"Ethan, it is yours, I haven't had sex with anyone else, you were the only one."

"I can't be a part of this, get out, Olive, I have Jessica now." He grabbed me by my wrist firmly, then pushed me out the living room door. Just as he was pushing me down the hallway, the front door swings open.

"Oh, hi, Olive. I didn't know you were coming over?"

"She's just leaving, Jessica," Ethan said calmly from behind me.

"Yeah, I'm just leaving. Just popped round to ask Ethan if I could use his phone to call someone as mines broke."

"Oh OK," Jessica said as I rushed past her, clutching tightly onto the scan photo that was in the palm of my sweaty hands.

I heard Jessica shout 'bye 'as I quickly jumped in my car. I rushed off the driveway and tears began to form in my eyes.

End of Flashback

I sat in the middle of the room, that empty feeling returning to my heart like it did that very day.

I flicked through the next pages seeing the first picture that was ever taken of Charles. I smiled because my child was the reason that I could survive the days that are called tomorrow.

After getting lost in my trail of thoughts, I managed to pry myself away from the photo album and head to bed.

Tomorrow is another day, I told myself as I drifted off to sleep.

I woke up the next day feeling lighter like the whole world had just floated from my shoulders. Rolling out of bed, I looked in the mirror and smiled at myself. I felt different, no worries, I felt carefree.

Maybe it wasn't such a bad thing to talk to people, I should have never listened to what he said because I'm not alone.

As I walked downstairs, the smell of bacon filled my nostrils making my mouth water. I rushed into the kitchen to see Tyler cooking breakfast and Charles happily sat in his pram playing with a toy, a toy I'd never seen before.

"Morning," I said to Tyler as I walked past her taking a seat at the table.

"More like afternoon." I took my phone out of my jean pocket to see that it had just gone midday.

"I'm sorry, I have overslept. Here, let me make breakfast." I ran over to Tyler, who just simply moved away from my actions.

"Don't be silly, you deserved to oversleep and this breakfast is a treat from me. So, get back over there and sit down." She laughed playfully.

I did as I was told and went back and sat at the table. When I got back to the seat, I had a blue-eyed baby looking right at me and I couldn't help but smile.

"Good morning, little one, how did you sleep?" I picked him out of his pram and cradled him in my arms.

"He slept just fine, now breakfast is severed." Tyler placed two full plates of food on the table.

"I thought I could do a mix and match breakfast and lunch. So, just eat what you feel like eating, have whatever you fancy." she smiled at me, handing me an empty plate.

Tyler, Charles and I sat around the table eating the delicious food in silence, just enjoying the moment.

That was until the doorbell rang.

I stood up to get the door, but Tyler hushed me and she went instead. The doorbell sounded one more time before the click of the lock indicated that Tyler had opened the door.

The house was silent, I could only just make out that a man was at the door by the tone of his voice.

Curiosity took over me and I slowly crept up behind the kitchen door and started listening to the conversation.

At first, I just heard a mumble, but then the more I focused, the voices became clear.

"Tyler, isn't it?" the male figure questioned.

"Yes, sir, you're the inspector that came to visit me not so long ago."

"Yes, this is correct. If I may ask, what are you doing at Miss Smith's residence?"

"I stayed the night. She's an old school friend, we lost contact but now I've moved back here, we got back in contact."

"I see. Is Miss Smith available to talk?" I moved away from the door; I could hear footsteps becoming louder in my direction. The next thing I knew was the kitchen door opened.

I panicked and turned around pretending to make up one of Charles' bottles.

"She's right in here, Inspector." Tyler looked at me and gave me an apologetic look.

"Miss Smith, nice to see you again."

"Nice to see you too, Inspector Brown, may I ask why you are here?"

"I'm here to ask you a few more questions and I would advise you to be careful when answering them." My palms became sweaty just hearing those words.

"Take a seat, Inspector," Tyler offered.

The inspector took a seat across the table from me, he set a bunch of papers out on the table. I tried to have a sly look at them but I couldn't see clearly enough.

Tyler grabbed Charles and made her way into the front room. I was glad she was here, I felt more relaxed, sort of.

As soon as she walked out of the kitchen, that's when everything changed.

"Olive, when was the last time you saw Ethan?"

"I saw him that morning."

"Why were you at his house the night of the murder?"

"I'm sorry, I don't remember being there."

"Olive, you were escorted out of the house by officers, then taken back to an ambulance to be checked over."

"That happened? I was actually in the back of an ambulance? So, the dreams are true." My mouth dropped open.

"What dreams? Olive, I need to know." The inspector pushed forward with his questions.

"I've been having these dreams since that night, like vague memories, but last night, I had one which was clearer," I answered my voice becoming shaky.

"What happened in the dream?"

"I was in a room, then a male figure walked towards me. He collapsed in my arms. My vision was blurred, I looked out the window then as I turned around to face the male figure, I caught a glimpse of myself in the mirror. After seeing myself, I felt weird, I didn't want to look down, I was scared. I forced myself to look down to see that his face was stained with blood and then the fresh blood trickled down the side of his face."

"Did you recognise the male?"

"No, the only person I recognised—" I stopped myself, I couldn't get myself to say her name.

"Recognise who?" the inspector looked intrigued.

"Jessica," I almost whispered.

"Jessica as in Ethan's partner?"

"Yes." My voice becoming barely audible.

"Is there any more to this dream?"

"Yes, I was holding his body, then the door to the room burst open and Jessica was stood there with an officer behind her. Then she started yelling at me 'what have you done?'. Then more officers appeared and began to restrain Jess from coming in any further. Once she was out of the room, I dropped his body, I felt empty like I had just lost my best friend. Two officers came over and collected me from the floor, that's all I can remember."

The inspector wrote something on his note pad, before picking up his phone and asking for backup.

"Miss Smith, you said his body and it was like losing your best friend?"

"I did." It was at that moment that I realised that the figure whom I held so tightly in my arms was Ethan.

"Ethan," I whispered. Then at that moment, everything went slow.

The last thing I heard was, "Miss Smith, you are under arrest for the murder of Ethan Davies." My world shattered into a million pieces.

Sirens bellowed through the house, the cold metal of handcuffs hit my wrists. I was dragged out of the kitchen to see a teary-eyed Tyler holding my baby.

I was pushed out of the front door of my own home, I looked back to see Tyler was now crying her tears glistening.

"Please take care of my baby. Tyler, you know me, I'm innocent," I shouted at the top of my lungs before I was put in the back of a police car.

"I will look after him, Olive and I know, I believe you." I heard her yell back as the door slammed shut in my face.

I let my hands fall into my lap, I couldn't control the tears anymore, they just spilt over the rims of my eyes.

My vision went blurred, my breathing became heavy. I felt like I was going to pass out.

"We are going to take her back to the station for more questioning," the officer said and for some reason, I recognised his voice.

He spun around to glance at me, then it hit me. He was the officer who walked in the room with Jessica.

The car started to move, I took one last glance behind me, at Tyler and Charles and the place I had made a home.

About a minute later, all of that was out of sight and I kept my head forward not wanting to move.

I felt like at any moment I would pass out. My heart quickened; I couldn't breathe. I felt like I was on fire then everything went black.

Chapter Three
The Interview

The lighting was dim and my eyes are stinging from my tears. I was sat in a room that had a cold feeling about it. My hands were handcuffed to the legs of the chair I was sat on.

I felt alone, I began to panic, my mind raced, my head hurts.

I sat there for a while before the door handle moved slightly and I jolted upright.

The inspector who removed me from my home walked in followed by another officer. Both took a seat opposite and stared right through my soul.

"Miss Smith, this will be a recorded interview," inspector Brown said.

"This is PC James, she will be accompanying me through this interview."

The stern woman reached down and pulled out a notebook, slamming it onto the table, then she grabbed a pen out of the top pocket of her shirt.

"20th August 2012. Interviewing Miss Olive Smith on the murder case of Ethan Davies. Miss Smith, you do not have to say anything, but it may harm your defence if you do not mention something which you later rely on in court. Anything you do say may be given as evidence. Where were you on the night of Ethan Davie's death?"

"I've already told you this," I shot back, confused as to why he was asking me something he already knew the answer to.

"I need you to tell me, Miss Smith."

"I drove to his house that evening."

"Why did you drive to his property, Miss Smith?."

"He wanted to talk to me in person."

"You didn't go there and intend to kill him? Did you argue?"

"What? No."

"How was your relationship with his partner, Mrs Davies?"

"Bumpy, but we became close."

"We have a statement which says that at their wedding, a few months prior to his death, you caused a scene by starting an argument with Jessica at their reception."

"It was not an argument; it was a slight misunderstanding. The seating arrangement had been changed last minute."

"Am I right when I say you have some hatred and jealousy towards Mrs Davies?"

"No, what are you on about?"

"Did you murder Ethan Davies because you were jealous? Did you murder him so Jessica Davies wouldn't be able to have him?"

"How dare you say that. I would never do anything like that. My god, something like that would never even cross my mind." I slammed my hands down on the table, tears burning my cheeks. The anger was building inside me like a pyramid.

I threw my head back and shut my eyes. I heard the inspector and the officer ruffling around the notes they hand taken.

All of a sudden, I heard a chair screech across the floor. My headshot forward and I don't know what came over me, but I blurted out.

"Whatever you have written about me, it best be the truth, you need to believe me, I'm a mother of a child. I would never harm anyone."

"Some people are innocent, some people aren't, Miss Smith, but in-between that fine line stands facts, evidence, statements and a long road of torture. Only at the end shall we see the results, but losing yourself won't get you anywhere." the inspector said as he headed out of the room.

"I'm going to get myself a lawyer, don't worry, I will fight for the truth," I shouted as he pushed the officer out of the room, slamming the door shut.

The room became silent as I replayed the words that stabbed right through my heart, 'Did you kill Ethan Davies?'.

Those five words echoed through the walls of my skull like a bell. I sat in silence looking around the room. How has it all come to this?

After twenty minutes, the door swung open and two officers walked in, removing my handcuffs from the legs of the chair, they then dragged my dull body out of the room.

Once outside the room, the lights burned my eyes. I was taken to the front of the station where I handed in everything from my pockets and anything that could be of a threat to the officers.

I stood at the desk, all the officers just stared right at me, I felt so small and empty.

After doing my fingerprints and signing some papers. I was then dragged to another room, where I was told to change into a plain white top and some simple grey joggers.

Minutes passed and I was dragged through hell, they showered me down, dressed me then finally put me behind a set of bars.

I slumped down on the metal bed. All that lay between my head and the cold metal is an overly used pillow, stained with many different memories.

Hours go by, I just lay there, cold and abandoned. My mind slips away into my cloud of thoughts. Tears gather at the corners of my eyes; I couldn't hold them back anymore.

Next thing I know is the droplets of steamy hot tears fall hard and fast. I covered my face with the pillow to try and drown out the sobs that escaped my quivering lips.

When the tears eventually stopped, I can't cry anymore. I sat up and watched as the guards laugh at each other's comments.

It was nice to see someone smile, but it stung when I realised that my little boy is with Tyler, not in my arms, smiling back at me with his ocean blue eyes.

Sitting there, I just continued to stare at their enjoyment until the officer in charge got up from her desk, walked over to the light on the wall.

"Lights out," she yelled, making me jump. She flicked the switch and the whole block went dead. I couldn't see.

Scared, I tucked myself under the thin sheet, which lay lightly over my shaken body.

Shadows roamed the hall, I didn't want to close my eyes. It has become too much for me, the stress from the events over the last forty-eight hours. Before I knew it, my eyes were shut.

"Wake up," a female voice rang through my ears.

My eyes fluttered open; the bright lights hurt my eyes as I sit up adjusting to my environment.

Moving off the bed, I made my way across the little box of a room to a tiny plastic mirror. Looking at my reflection, I felt disgusted with myself. As a mother, I doubted myself instantly.

Sitting back on the edge of the bed, I stared plainly at the wall regretting my decisions in life. I should never have felt so strongly about him, it was wrong, who am I?

An hour or two passed by before a guard stood outside my cell and yelled at me to stand up. I placed my hands behind my back. I do as I was told because I had no idea what would happen if I didn't co-operate.

I stood there, not allowing any emotion to slide upon my face. The metal gate opened and the guard walked in. As she walked behind me, I could feel the cold metal hit my skin.

"Walk forward," she demanded.

I stumbled forward, looking down the long halls which are filled with people.

"Turn left." I could feel the officer's presence right behind me. As I turned left, another officer stood up from the desk and stood right in front of me.

"Follow the officer in front of you and don't try anything. Just remember there are more of us than there is of you." She whispered the last sentence in my ear sending shivers down my spine.

Before I could reply, her hands pressed against my shoulders, then she began to push me forward taking me by surprise.

As we walked down the halls of cells, her words began to repeat in my head, 'There are more of us than there is of you. ' I was scared.

The further we headed down the halls, the more people I began to see. Most of them laid their heads against the bars. The other half pleaded for someone to listen to them, others just sat starring at walls in silence.

We came to a door at the end of the hall. The officer in front opened the door wide to reveal another hallway, but this one was much smaller.

After about ten minutes, the officers finally released their grip on me.

"Miss Smith, you are going to have another interview," the inspector said as he got off his chair and pointed to a door across the other end of the office.

A pair of hands made their way back to my shoulders, their grip tightened before I was yet again pushed forward.

The door to the interview room opened and I was forced to sit back in the same chair I was sat in yesterday.

The officer took my hands and then handcuffed them to the legs of the chair.

I was then left alone, the officer left me in the room to wait for the inspector. I didn't understand why he wants to interview me again. I've told him everything.

Whilst I was waiting for the inspector, I managed to get lost in my thoughts. I was lost in the thought that some of the people in the cells could be innocent, but how can they prove that they are? How can I prove to them I am? Because I am innocent, but how do you prove your innocence?

My thoughts were interrupted by the opening of the door. The inspector walked over and took a seat at the table, but this time, he did not have another officer with him.

"I would like to ask you a few more questions."

"Why haven't you got another officer with you?"

"Because this isn't an official interview, it's just a simple questioning." the inspector said as he lay paper across the table.

"Oh," was all I managed to say.

The inspector glanced over the pieces of paper, furrowing his eyebrows as he came to stop at one particular piece.

"The night you went to Ethan's house, why were you going there?"

"I have told you this, I went to his house because he wanted to talk to me about something."

"What was the first thing you remember about that night?" he questioned before writing something down in his note pad.

"I remember receiving a phone call from Ethan asking me to come round his."

"What was said on the phone?"

"Not much, all he said was he needs to speak to me as soon as possible. I asked him to tell me over the phone, but he said he had to tell me in person."

"What did he seem like on the phone, was he acting differently to how he would normally speak over the phone?"

"Yes, actually come to think of it, he sounded worried."

"After the phone call, what did you do?"

"I put a coat on, then jumped straight in my car and went right over to his house."

"How far do you live away from Ethan?"

"About twenty-five to thirty minutes away."

"Interesting, what time did you arrive at the property?"

"I arrived at about twenty past nine."

"So, not too long before his murder took place, did you go straight into the house?"

"I sat in my car for about ten minutes, the house was pitch black. I wasn't sure what was going on, there are normally lights on."

"So, would you say the scene was out of place? When did you decide to go in?"

"Now I've thought about it, it was unusual to arrive and for them to have no lights on, especially when he phoned me to come over. I was going to drive off, but Ethan messaged saying he could see the car and to just walk in, he would be in the kitchen." The inspector took a moment to process what I just said.

"Thank you for co-operating with me. I will be back in a minute. I just need to speak to someone and sort some things out." He relined the papers in his hands, then left the room, leaving me to be consumed by my thoughts.

As time caught up with me, I began to think back to that night. Why couldn't I remember anything that happened from the time I entered the house, but I remembered holding his body. What happened in between?

"Sorry, I took so long," the inspector entered the room. I noticed he no longer had the pieces of paper that he originally had bought in. Instead, he had what looked like a pile of photographs.

The inspector pulled his chair out from beneath the table and softly placed the photographs in front of himself, but he made sure to hide the images with a sheet of paper.

"I would like to show you some of these images and I want you to say what you think." He slowly revealed the first image, my breath hitched in my throat when I saw it.

"That's Ethan's body?" Tears flowed freely with my words.

"Yes, now from what you told me earlier, a witness has verified your statement and what you have told me is true. You are no longer a subject of interest, but I would be grateful if you would help solve Ethan's murder. Just tell me as much as you can." His word hit me hard, I couldn't believe that I was a prime suspect.

"Wait, why am I here if I'm not a prime suspect anymore?"

"I need to show you some images to see if anything can help you remember what happened in the space you blacked out." The inspector slid multiple images across the open space of the table. I froze as I saw the horrific images that lay in front of me.

"Miss Smith, these are photographs taken at the scene of Ethan's death, there are images of you in here," he said as he pushed a photograph forward so that it was directly in my view.

"Whose blood is that on my skin and shirt?" I stuttered.

"That is Ethan's. Do you remember how you got his blood all over you?" All I could do was shake my head in response.

"When we arrived at the scene, you were laying on his bedroom floor, holding him in your arms. You whispered something to him." I shook my head becoming frustrated with myself because I was trying so hard and I still couldn't remember.

"Why did you think I murdered him, you have no evidence?" I let that slip out of my mouth without thinking.

"We had been told by someone that you murdered him, yes, we have no evidence. There wasn't any at the scene. Miss Smith we are trying to solve this mystery and any suspicions have to be investigated. You were close with Ethan and at the property at the time of death."

"So, you took me away from my son without investigating that person's extremely bold statement about me?" Anger boiled through my veins.

"We had investigated the statement and the majority of it had been proven. So, we had no other reason to believe otherwise until this morning when someone clarified your statement."

Silence filled the room as I took in everything that had just been said. Who would say I murdered Ethan? Everyone who knew us knew we had been childhood friends since day one.

"I understand this is a lot to take in and believe me, Miss Smith, everyone makes mistakes otherwise they wouldn't be human. It was just my job to make sure that the murderer does not get away with taking away someone's life," the inspector said, breaking the thick silence that ventilated the room.

"I understand." I looked down at the images, then back up at the inspector.

"I need you to help me out for a little longer, is that OK?"

"Yes, but after this, am I free to go?"

"Of course. Now all these images are from that night and I'm going to need you to think really hard about what happened," he said, spreading the images out so I could see them better.

"This one, I remember this." I pulled an image from underneath the pile on the table. The image was me in the back of an ambulance being examined.

"I have a different top on here?" I questioned.

"You had to be undressed, your other top was used for evidence. Do you remember this?" He pushed another image forward; the image was a picture of someone's head.

"This is your head. Do you remember falling or even hitting your head at any point?"

"I don't," I just stared blankly back at him across the table.

"What is the very last thing you remember before you woke up in the ambulance?"

"I remember speaking to Ethan in the kitchen."

"What were you speaking about?"

"About Charles."

"What about Charles?"

"About the labour plan, I was very close and Ethan wanted to be there, but rough times had left us drifting apart from each other."

"Rough times?"

"We argued about Charles." I felt so ashamed of myself, all those words that played through my mind of the bad arguments we had about Charles, now I can't take those stubborn words back.

"Why would you argue about Charles?"

"Ethan…is Charles' father." The words fell so easily out of my mouth, easier than I thought they would.

"Now it adds up. What did he want to talk about that night?"

"He wanted to talk about being at the birth, he said he had to be there. He mentioned something about he'd had this fight with his demons and he could see what he wanted more clearly. I still don't understand what he meant by that. I was trying to process what he said because after weeks on end of drowning in emotions, everything lifted when he let those words slip his lips."

"I see. When did the conversation end? Was Jessica present?"

"It was just him and me."

"Thank you for your co-operation with me, Miss Smith. I guess you have been waiting to hear these words since the time you got here. You are free to leave." He stood up and took the handcuffs from my wrists and set me free.

I stood up and walked out the door. The inspector led me to the front of the building where I then had to sit and wait for papers to be signed before I could be released.

As I sat there, I watched a mixture of deep reds and pinks collide with the blackness of the night sky that was starting to roll in.

"Miss Smith?" a male caught my attention. I stood up and walked towards the receptionist.

"Hi," I said as I approached the glass window.

"Here are the items that were removed from you. If you could just sign the bottom of this paper please, it's only your release form to say you are happy with the circumstances of us letting you go."

"Thank you." I grabbed the pen and scribbled my signature without hesitation.

Walking out of the station into the cold air of the night, I pulled out my phone and quickly dialled Tyler's number.

"Hey, this is Tyler."

"Hi, Tyler, it's me Ol—" I didn't even have time to finish my sentence before Tyler screeched down the phone.

"Olive, you're OK?"

"Yeah, I'm fine, look I was wondering if you could pick me up?"

"Yeah, sure, I will be right there, see you in ten minutes."

Whilst I waited for Tyler, I sat on a wall and just listened to the silence that I had missed so much, the silence that surrounded my freedom.

I could feel the air blow through my fingertips, I let my head relax back, sighing heavily.

It took roughly ten minutes before I saw Tyler's headlights run along the road. Her car pulled up alongside me, I heard her unlock the doors and climbed in without wanting to spend another second in the cold.

"Hi, where's Charles?" I asked looking over my shoulder at the empty seats.

"He's with Ethan's mum." Tyler kept her eyes focused forward, her tone of voice sheepish like she was hiding something.

"Why is he there?" I questioned Tyler as her behaviour became suspicious.

"I left him to bond with his grandmother," she said looking away.

"You told her?" I asked in utter shock.

"No, I wouldn't do that, you know I would never do that, right?"

"Right, how long has he been there?"

"He's been there since this morning; I had a job interview that I forgot about because everything happened so fast."

"That's fine, let's go get him."

"Yeah, about that, Susan wants to have him overnight, to let you rest."

"Oh, OK."

The rest of the car journey back was silent, not a word was said.

We arrived back. The house was barely visible. All the lights in the house were off, making the entrance to the house feel cold and abandoned. I just walked right into the front room and sat on the sofa dragging my hands down my face.

"What did the inspector ask you?" Tyler's voice made me jump as she took a seat next to me.

"He asked me a bunch of questions to do with Ethan's case. Someone had put me forward as a suspect and because I was there that night at the scene, I had become a prime suspect."

"Wait, you're kidding me, it's been months since he's passed, surely they would have done this at the start because you were at the scene, they should have sorted this out ages ago." She sighed heavily.

"I know, I just don't know who would do such a thing as to try and have me done for my best friend's murder."

Tyler and I sat there in the pitch black in silence. I could feel my eyes becoming heavy and I was also pretty sure that I heard a little yawn escape Tyler's lips.

"You can go home, Tyler, it's getting late," I said turning on the side lamp.

"You think I'm going home?" She looked at me and smiled.

"I didn't think you would stay."

"Of course, I'm not letting you sleep alone now, after everything you have been through, Olive. I'm not leaving again, that was my biggest mistake. I have learned that life is like a candle, it burns for so long before it burns out. So, Olive, I'm staying."

Tyler got up, walked out into the hallway and bought back in with her a suitcase. I just smiled at her actions.

"Thank you, Tyler, for everything." I stood up and hugged her fragile body in mine. For the first time in a while, I felt wanted, I felt like I had a purpose.

"What do you say we go to sleep now?" she said breaking the hug.

"We don't want you being tired when we go pick Charles up tomorrow morning, do we?" She smiled at me before heading out of the front room and making her way to bed.

After Tyler left the room, I turned off the side lamp then made my way upstairs. I couldn't wait to just get back into my own bed, even if it was for one night that I didn't sleep in it.

As I lay in bed, I thought about what Tyler said about life being like a candle and how things can change with the click of a finger.

It didn't take long for me to fall asleep; I was too tired from the events of the last twenty-four hours that I drifted away peacefully.

A bang startled me awake, I jumped out of bed exiting my bedroom slowly. I noticed a strip of light escaping from the side of the back room's door.

I walked with caution towards it. I pressed my face in the opening of the door and peeked in. I was shocked to see Tyler sat on the computer chair staring intensely at a photo frame.

"Tyler, are you OK?" Opening the door, I swiftly walked towards her and rested my hand upon her shoulder. "Why did

Ethan have to go? Out of all of us, he's the only one of us who hasn't done any wrongs in life and he went first."

I could hear her sniffle and I could see the droplets of her tears hit the floor. I moved around her body, so I could face her. She looked up, her bloodshot eyes trying to make contact with mine.

I put her hand in mine and tried to reassure her. "Tyler, he's in a better place now."

"I know, I just never expected anything to be this way."

"No one did, Tyler, it's just something unexpected." I felt sorry for Tyler, I never knew how heartbroken she was.

"I'm sorry, Olive. I've just never really thought about it. I wasn't here when it happened, I had a different life. I never realised how much I've missed everything until I came back home seeing you and Ethan's mum. I didn't realise how much I've missed out on."

Tyler wiped the following tears from her cheeks before standing up and letting a small smile appear on her face.

"Tyler, I understand it has hit you hard, but why didn't you say anything to me?" I stood up following her actions.

"You have got enough on your plate, Olive and I know you've had your time to grieve. You became mentally strong enough to pull yourself back up, I didn't want to bring you down again."

"You would have never bought me down, Tyler, you would have helped me. It's nice to know I have someone to talk about it to, I had no one, but now you're here, we have each other."

Tyler and I made our way downstairs into the kitchen. I grabbed two cups off the side of the unit and switched on the kettle.

"Go sit down," I told Tyler as I pointed at the table and chairs down the far end of the kitchen. Tyler just nodded and sat at the table.

I waited for the kettle to boil before pouring the hot liquid into the cups. I took a quick glance over Tyler before squeezing the tea bags against the side of the cups.

"Here you go." I placed Tyler's tea next to her, but her eyes didn't move from the peaceful scenery that was reflected through the window.

"Tyler, can I ask you something?" I had never really asked about her husband since she came back.

"Hmm," she mumbled, turning to face me and wrapping her fingers around the hot cup.

"How come you never talk about your husband since you have been back?" It was a risky question to ask, but I would never know unless I asked.

"I don't know. He just never came up in conversation."

Something was off with Tyler the second I asked about her husband, but I didn't want to be that person who asks too deeply into things.

"What's his name?" I asked casually taking a sip of my tea.

"Harrison."

"How did you two meet?"

"We met at a Christmas market just after I moved away." I couldn't tell whether or not to carry on. Her face told two different emotions.

"How long have you been together?"

"Well, I moved away in the last year of school, so I was just turning sixteen. He was in the year above us turning eighteen. We got together when I turned seventeen. That

Christmas, we bumped into each other at the market, where he asked for my number. We started talking, then we went on a date and he asked me to be his girlfriend. So, now we are in our twenties, I'd say about four years this December."

"What made you guys decide to get married?"

"We decided after two years, we were happy and content."

Tyler paused halfway through her sentence and her smile was quickly replaced with a frown. I thought it was best just to end that conversation as I didn't want to bring up the past when she could tell me in her own time.

We sat in silence, about ten minutes passed before Tyler yawned and decided to head back to bed.

Something was off with Tyler, she just got up and went to bed without saying goodnight.

I woke up the next morning rubbing my sleepy eyes and letting a slight yawn part my dry lips. I got up and dressed, decided on wearing a pair of baby blue jeans that hugged my hips perfectly with a plain white t-shirt.

After I had got myself ready for the day, I exited my bedroom and walked across the hallway to look over up at the spare bedroom to see Tyler's door wide open. Her body was spread across the top of the unmade bed sheets.

I debated on waking her up, but I thought back to last night and just let her sleep in peace.

As I made my way downstairs, I thought about what Tyler told me last night about her husband and the way she reacted when she spoke about him.

Tyler's emotions last night were dry; it's like something happened and she didn't know how to feel, it was like she is numb.

I had been so deep in my thoughts I didn't realise that I was stood in the middle of the kitchen. I was unable to recall how I had made my way downstairs.

I sat at the window drinking a cup of tea and I just took in the silence. The peaceful scene that laid on the other side of the glass window calmed me and drowned out my thoughts of the recent events.

I watched as the deep blues of the sky reflect on the clear ocean surface, the waves slightly swaying as there was only a small breeze that brushed through the long grass.

I touched the window and felt the cold collide with my fingertips. I shut my eyes and took in a deep breath. When I opened my eyes, I decided that whilst Tyler is asleep and Charles was still at his nan's house, I would spend the remaining time to myself.

I left Tyler a note to say that I had gone for a walk and that I would be back soon. Then I pulled a coat over my body and made my way out the front door.

The light breeze flowed through the ends of my hair whilst the sun beamed off my skin. I felt relaxed and alone but this time, I was happy to be alone.

I walked further down the beach right up to the edge of the water. I looked down at the crystal-clear water that layered itself thinly just before my shoes.

I stood there staring at the water that was coming and going freely, then slipped off my shoes and socks. I let my bare skin touch the gritted sand, then edged my way forward until my feet made contact with the icy cold water.

I felt so free, not a worry in the world like every problem that was sat in the walls of my mind had dissolved.

The sun shone across the sea creating a ripple of colour, the water had made my feet slightly numb.

The breath-taking view left me stunned for a while before I turned and looked back at the house that stood so proudly amongst the fields.

After about an hour, I decided to head back to the house. I was positive that Tyler would be awake by now.

Chapter Four

A Loyal Friendship

Opening the front door, I noticed the house still lay in silence. I walked into the kitchen to see that the note I had left for Tyler had been taken.

I decided to go to Tyler's room, she was obviously awake. Making my way upstairs, I heard a faint sob. The conversations of last night came back to mind as I edged closer to the room. I opened the door to see Tyler sat on the edge of the bed, her eyes bloodshot from crying, her hair messy from the stressful emotions.

"Tyler?" I said whilst pushing the door open slightly, but she didn't answer me.

"Tyler what's wrong?" This time she lifted her head revealing the tears that had burned her cheeks. I moved closer to her unsure of whether she wanted me in her presence or not.

"You can come in, I need to talk to you." After those words left her mouth, I sat next to her letting a reassuring smile settle upon my face.

"What's up?" She looked at me with many expressions crossing over her skin within seconds.

"I need to tell you everything. I was the one who told you to talk about things and here I am keeping secrets, emotions and memories locked away from you." What she said took me by surprise. I wanted so desperately to comfort her in a warm embrace, but I was scared of what would come from her lips next.

"OK, let's start, better out than in." I giggled trying to lighten the mood, but she just stared back at me with dull eyes. I knew from that moment that this wasn't the happy Tyler I once knew; something was truly wrong.

"Remember I told you I moved here with my husband, Harrison?"

"Yeah."

"Well, I didn't I moved away from him," she said, bowing her head down in shame.

"What? Why?" I asked, obviously confused as to why she would lie about this.

"Thing's happened between Harrison and me, bad things." Her hands began to tremble as she spoke, I could tell she was scared.

"Bad things?" I said, feeling scared to know what had happened.

"He became overprotective but abusive. I don't really want to talk about it, I don't feel strong enough."

"Why didn't you say?"

"When I first saw you in town, it bought back memories, which carried a happy feeling. I hadn't felt like that for years, so that's why I never said anything."

"I understand that feeling, but how come you came back here?"

"This was the only place I knew. So, I remembered that at Ethan's funeral Susan gave me her number, so I've been living with her for a few months. Due to things that happened with Harrison and me, I never really have left her house and I asked her to keep quiet."

"Wait, so you went to Ethan's funeral? How did you get Susan's number? How did she know you were there?"

So many questions flew through my mind, it was becoming hard to focus and take everything in.

"Harrison agreed I could go, but I was not allowed to be seen, but Susan saw me standing behind a blue car waiting for everyone to leave. She came over to me and spoke. She looked at Harrison then back at me, then handed me Ethan's memorial card."

"I wondered why she went over to a blue car. It was you."

This whole conversation had my head in a huge mess.

"Susan didn't say anything, she just looked inside the car and I knew she watched Harrison grabbing my arm because she went wide-eyed and she saw the bruises that lay upon my skin."

"I'm so sorry, Tyler, I can't imagine what you have been through." Emotions collided, I felt angry, sad and confused.

"It wasn't until I got home that I realised that Susan had left her number and a note on the back of Ethan's memorial card."

"What did the note say?"

"It said, 'I know what's going on, Tyler, run away and come to me.' I don't know how she knew what I was going through, the only person who knew was—" Tyler froze before she could finish her sentence.

"Susan was in an abusive relationship with Ethan's father and who else did you tell? You could have told me?"

"That's how she knew, she could see the signs. I never told you because I couldn't, I don't know why but I just didn't want to put any of my problems on you, you had just lost your mum and the person whom I told was…I don't want to say because it will look bad me telling them and not you."

"Tyler, I'm not going to be annoyed."

"I told Ethan and Jessica." My blood began to boil as Jessica's name slipped past Tyler's lips.

"You told Jessica before me?" I felt betrayed, Tyler began to cry before placing her hand on my shoulder to try and get me to focus.

"Olive, she just turned up, Ethan had seen Harrison hit me outside the hotel that we stayed at. I went back to Ethan's house and of course, Jessica had already moved in with him. He couldn't just say, I showed up all teary-eyed for no reason."

"I don't know what to say? This is a lot to take in."

"I understand I should have told you sooner."

"Is that it or is there more?" I said.

"Yeah, there is more and to be honest, if you thought what I told you was a shock, then I'm dreading how you will react when I tell you the next part," Tyler said, her eyes shining with guilt.

"I think I can cope now, Tyler." I laughed nervously.

"Well here goes nothing." Tyler took in a deep breath before looking over her right shoulder directly at me.

"I was there the night of Ethan's murder; I was at the house." The last part of the sentence became muffled as Tyler spoke.

My head felt heavy. I looked down at my hands, feeling numb like my body parts were no longer connected. Then I looked over towards Tyler who was speaking to me, but I couldn't hear anything she was saying, all I could hear was this high-pitched whistle that echoed from ear to ear.

My whole world just slowed right down.

"Olive, I swear I didn't know Ethan was going to be murdered, Jessica called me to come over after she had finished work. She told me she had something important to tell me, but I didn't know what it was." I could hear Tyler's words starting to become clear again.

"I'm so confused, Tyler. If you were there that night, you would know who killed him?" Tyler looked over at me, she knew something, she had guilt written all over her face.

"I killed him, didn't I?"

"No, Olive, you didn't."

"How do you know?"

"I saw you holding him, but he was dying before he got to you."

"Who killed him?" Anger pulsing through my veins.

"I don't know. I have told the inspector all that I know."

Everything was slowly starting to make sense now. Tyler was that person who verified my statement and helped me prove my innocence.

"Did you come to the station and tell them that I wasn't the one who killed Ethan?"

"Yes, I never told them about where I was because I was never asked."

"How didn't they see you at the property?"

"I got scared, I walked into the kitchen to talk to Jessica and Ethan was covered in blood."

"Didn't they see you?"

"No, I don't think so. All I can remember was the two of them having an argument over an unborn child. Then I got scared when I saw the blood dripping down Ethan's face. After I saw his face, I quickly walked out of the house being careful not to make a noise."

"But you told Ethan you were coming around?"

"Once I was out of the house, I messaged him saying I couldn't make it. I told him that something came up between Harrison and me."

The room fell silent, neither of us knew what to say. It felt like a massive puzzle that was starting to fall into place from the events that haunted this town.

The silence in the room was broken by the vibration of my phone in my jean pocket. I looked at the caller ID and noticed it was Susan.

Then it hit me that she still had Charles and Tyler and I said we would pick him up this morning. Then I looked at the time to see it was midday, crap!

"Hello," I said shyly as I answered the call.

"Hi, Olive, I was just wondering when you would be picking Charles up? Is everything OK?"

"Yeah, I will pick him up soon."

"It's not a bother if you need me to have him for longer." Susan could sense that something wasn't right.

"Actually, Susan if you don't mind, could you have Charles until later this afternoon?"

"Of course, I was planning on taking him out for picnic. So, it's not a problem."

"Thank you, Susan." I sighed heavily in relief.

"Anytime and, Olive, I need to talk to you soon, so whenever you're free, could you pop around?"

"Yeah, no problem." I wondered what she would like to talk about, but at this stage, I'm thinking it could literally be anything.

I put the phone down and turned to face Tyler once again. Her face looked tired and worn down.

"So, anything else you want to tell me?" I asked Tyler, her lazy eyes scanning over my face.

"Yeah. Remember that day I folded the pram and made it look really easy?"

"Yes, and I made that comment and your mood just flew out the window."

"Well, I have a child. I mean had a child." Tears for the second time this morning formed along Tyler's eyes.

"What do you mean had?"

"Her name was Lola, she died in a car crash."

"Tyler, I'm so sorry, how old was she?"

"She was one, it was actually the day of her first birthday." Tyler just stared into thin air; you could see she was reminiscing on the memories she shared with her child.

"How did it happen? Don't tell me if you're not comfortable saying." I didn't want to push her, this must be horrible for her.

"I asked Harrison to go out and get some last-minute party food whilst I prepared for the party."

"Wait, so Harrison was driving the car?"

"Yeah, he offered to take her with him to have some bonding time with her as he hadn't been home much."

"Why hadn't he been home much?"

"He said he was working late, but I thought different. He smelt of women's perfume every time he came home."

"He was cheating on you?"

"Yeah, that's what I believe anyway."

I couldn't believe what I was hearing. I felt so guilty for not being able to do anything. I felt useless.

"Olive, I'm glad I have told you this. I feel so much better for getting things off my chest and I don't feel so bad for telling you to get everything off your chest, we are equal now."

Tyler let a small smile creep upon her lips. This was the first time I had seen Tyler smile properly since I was released from the police station.

"Shall we go have some lunch because I think we missed the breakfast period," I said earning a little giggle from Tyler.

I made my way out of the room leaving Tyler in peace to get dressed and freshen herself up. Walking downstairs, I felt a weight lifted from my shoulders. I was happy to actually help Tyler by listening to her secrets that she had bottled up in her body's temple.

I remembered what Tyler had done for me the other day and decided to repay her by creating a wonderful buffet.

I started by slicing the lettuce and fruits, then mixing them in a glass bowl so that the different colours mixed together.

I walked over to the fridge, grabbed out the fresh ham and placed it alongside the bowl of fruits and lettuce.

The smell of the delicious foods filled the kitchen making my mouth water. Tyler must have smelt the food because she rushed down the stairs into the kitchen.

She walked over to the unit next to me and just looked at the food I'd laid out.

"This all smells amazing," Tyler said, breathing in heavily through her nostrils.

"Indeed, it does, can't wait to eat it," I replied, continuing to do the same actions as Tyler.

Tyler went and sat at the table and I placed down the different foods. It didn't take her long before she had tucked into the food that I had prepared.

Placing the last of the food on the table, I took a seat across from Tyler. We sat in silence, one of us occasionally looking up to smile at each other. It was almost like what we had spoken about was now unspoken.

The sun beamed through the clouds, the heat of the sun hitting our skin through the window.

"After this, shall we go pick up Charles?" Tyler Said with her mouth half full of food.

"Yeah." I thought about Charles and about over the last few hours, I had forgotten about his presence but not completely.

About half an hour after we had eaten and cleaned everything up, we climbed into Tyler's car and then set off in the direction of Susan's house to pick up Charles.

The car journey felt slow; it couldn't have gone any slower. We drove for about an hour before arriving at Susan's front door, excitement fuelled my body until I remembered that Susan wanted to talk to me.

Tyler knocked on the door and it took seconds for Susan to answer. Walking in the house, memories of my childhood flooded back.

"Look who's here, Charles," Susan said, Charles' small laugh echoed through my ears filling my heart with joy.

Tyler and I walked into the front room to see Charles wiggling around on a plain white blanket with some new toys.

I took the pleasure of picking Charles up and holding him close to my chest. Feeling his tiny body against mine brought back the memories that created our mother and son bond. I could feel him wrap his tiny fingers around my thumb.

"Hello, mummy is back now and she's never letting go of you again," I said, my speech muffled due to the close proximity of my mouth against the top of his fragile head.

"Olive, can I talk to you?" Susan said as she walked towards the hall entrance.

"Tyler, can you keep an eye on Charles?" Tyler walked over to me, but before she could take Charles out of my grasp, Susan spoke up.

"Tyler, you will be included in this conversation too, Charles will be fine where he is," she said with such a dead tone voice leaving Tyler and me apprehensive.

After Susan spoke, she left the room, her body language gave away nothing about the conversation we were about to have. Tyler and I followed Susan into her kitchen giving a quick 'what's this about 'look before settling down at the dining room table.

"Susan, what's this about?" Tyler was the first one to break the silence by asking the question we both wanted answered.

"Ethan," she simply replied.

"What about Ethan?" I asked, not wanting Tyler to ask all the questions.

"There are secrets, secrets that everyone holds, but we need to piece what we are all hiding together."

Tyler and I sat there in confusion. What did she mean by piecing together our secrets?

Seconds passed before the penny finally dropped.

Tyler and I turned towards each other and realised what Susan was on about. Susan knew Tyler and I had been talking.

"What do you want to know?" Tyler asks.

"Why you left for the police station to free Olive and what you said the proved her innocence?"

"I went there because I knew Olive was innocent."

"How?" Susan pressed on.

"I just know." I didn't understand why Tyler wasn't telling Susan what she told me. But whilst Tyler was becoming stubborn, Susan began to break her emotions slowly started coming out.

"I said how," Susan raised her voice, indicating to Tyler that she was on the edge of blowing.

"I was at Ethan's house the time he was killed," Tyler let out. Susan just sat there in shock.

"I went there to talk to Jessica about something, she said she wanted to tell me something important."

"Why did you leave?" Susan fired back with a question.

"I heard Jessica screaming at Ethan, then all of a sudden he came into view in the front room window." Tyler's face went pale. She did not want to tell his mother the next part, but she knew she had too. Susan had the right to know.

"Susan, I don't want to upset you, but I want you to know everything only because you have the right to know." Susan's facial expressions changed from angry to worried.

"When Ethan came into sight, I saw blood dripping down his face, he looked scared and like he'd been betrayed."

The words left Tyler's mouth, then tears slip down Susan's pale skin. Her lips began to tremble, it was like she had dreamt of this moment but never felt the real pain that stung her heart.

"I'm so sorry, Susan," Tyler said, feeling awful but relieved at the same time.

"It's not your fault," was all Susan could get out.

Susan stood up from the dining table, leaving Tyler and me feeling so guilty. She walked over to where the kettle sat and flipped the switch.

"Tea?"

"Yes," Tyler and I said in unison.

The room was so silent, the only noise that could be heard was the water in the kettle bubbling around as the water and heat collided.

Tyler and I watched patiently as Susan poured the hot liquid into the cups. Susan looked so fragile, but then I guess she had just heard about what her son looked like moments before passing and she wasn't there to save him.

Thinking about how Susan reacted made me feel small. It got me thinking about what if it was Charles and me in that situation. I couldn't bear to think about it anymore.

"Here you go." Susan placed the hot cups in front of the two of us, then sat back down herself.

"Tyler, why didn't you help him?" The pain of losing her son shone through her voice.

"Um…well, I was scared, I froze, I didn't know what to do." Tyler fumbled with her words.

As Tyler was speaking, I remembered her saying that she saw me holding Ethan. I didn't realise she saw him before that. What is she still hiding? I need to know.

"Tyler, you told me you saw me holding Ethan, why didn't you mention seeing him before?" You could see the concentration on Tyler's face as she thought back to that chat we had this morning.

"I forgot that I saw him." Tyler seemed genuine.

"I saw him in the front room, then he made his way to the other room where you were." Tyler's eyebrows were knitted together as she tried to remember every little detail.

"What? Why were you holding him?" Susan looked over at me speaking before I could reply to Tyler.

"Ethan, he called me asking to come round and talk about us," I said, a lump forming in my throat as I remembered the phone call.

"About us?" Susan tilted her head to indicate she was confused.

"We had been arguing over something." I looked at Tyler for help, but she turned to me sending me a 'you have to do this one on your own 'look. I sighed heavily.

"Susan, Charles is Ethan's." I watched as her face filled with a whole load of emotions.

"I thought Charles was Ethan's child, but I never believed it. I thought you would have told me." She sounded hurt.

"It was hard to tell you and hard not to tell you," I said softly.

"He never told me." Susan burst into tears, sadness filled the room as the mother of a deceased son let out her pain.

"Susan, why did you ask Tyler and me to come here and tell you things you already knew?"

"I wanted to hear it, that's all. I needed to hear you say it before I could believe."

"Is there anything else?" Tyler said. You could sense she was getting uncomfortable.

"Tyler, did you see anyone else there?"

"All I could see was Ethan and Olive. I knew Jessica was there because I could hear her." Tyler verified Susan's question.

Susan looked happy with what Tyler and I had told her. We all sat there in silence, not one of us making eye contact, but you could see the feelings of memories floating around.

"I'm going to see my child now." I stood up making my way out of the kitchen.

"I will make us all some snacks," Susan said, leaving Tyler sat at the table on her own.

"I will go back into the front room with Olive." Tyler stood up. Moments later, she joined me on the floor with Charles.

I just sat there smiling at the one thing that kept my life in a straight order. His smile could light up any room within seconds.

"I'm glad we spoke about everything," I said, looking at Tyler.

"And me, I feel relieved."

We both sat there smiling, feeling accomplished with how far we both had come through everything.

Charles began to cry, interrupting the silence that sat in the room. I picked him up and got up off the floor, took a seat on the same old sofa that I sat upon as a child.

"Food is served." Susan walked over handing Tyler and myself a plate with nibbles on it.

Susan sat next to me and switched on the TV. I had noticed that Tyler hadn't moved from her space on the living room floor, she just sat there as white as a ghost.

"Tyler, are you all right?" Concern overwhelming my body.

"Huh, yeah, I'm fine."

"Why are you still sat on the floor?" I giggled.

"I don't know." She nervously laughed back.

Susan took Charles off me so I could eat my food. Whilst eating my food, I carefully watched Tyler, something wasn't right with her. I felt like asking her, but her body language told me not to bother.

The afternoon flew by and it became dark outside. It had been a long day, Charles was becoming tired and so was I.

"Tyler, you staying at mine again?" Her head shot up and her eyes held a horrid story.

"As long as you're OK with that. I feel like a burden staying here with Susan all the time."

"It's not a bother, I don't mind. You're an adult now, you make your own decisions." Susan said, patting Tyler's shoulders.

"Then if it's OK, I'm going to stay at Olive's," Tyler said, standing up on her feet and smiling over at me.

"That's fine," Susan said, moving her body towards the hallway.

I collected Charles' things, double-checking I had everything. Then Tyler and I made our way out to the car.

We got in the car and I watched as Tyler didn't look back, she just kept her eyes forward. The engine fired up as the car started. I waved goodbye to Susan as we left for my house.

About halfway home, I turned my head to see Charles peacefully asleep in his car seat.

We arrived at the house, the night sky had completely drawn in now, the air was cold making Tyler and I shiver as we exited the car.

The house was cold and dark. I placed Charles straight in his cot as soon as we got in, not wanting to disturb him.

After putting him to bed. I went downstairs to see if Tyler wanted to watch a film after the long day we have had. When I got to the front room, which is where I last saw her, she was not there.

I walked back upstairs to see the light shining on the floor outside the spare bedroom. Pushing the door open, I could see Tyler in bed.

"Tyler, is everything OK? I thought we could watch a film after the long day we've had."

"Not tonight, Olive, I just don't feel well and I want to sleep."

I just smiled at Tyler before turning on my heels, switched the bedroom light off and whispered goodnight as I shut the door.

Collapsing onto my bed, I let my body relax and the tiredness got the better of me. Before I knew it, I was asleep.

"Olive," Tyler screamed.

I jumped out of bed, adrenaline pumping through my body. I rushed out of my bedroom. Tyler's door was wide open. I ran into the room, the smell of sick making my stomach curdle.

I looked at Tyler, you could practically see through her. She had thrown up all over the bedsheets. She looked dead.

"Tyler, what's wrong? What happened?" I grabbed her wrist checking her pulse, but I could barely pick anything up. Her body began to relax, but she wasn't reacting.

"Tyler, can you hear me?" I moved her head slightly, she was super-hot. Without hesitation, I ran to get my phone, then rushed back to her side.

The dial tone rang for what felt like forever.

"Hello, 999, what service do you require?"

"Ambulance."

"What's happened?"

"My friend, she's not responding, she's hot and she's thrown up all over herself."

"Have you checked her pulse? Has she got a pulse?"

"Barely." I began to cry.

"An ambulance is on its way. I need you to stay on the line until the crew are with you, OK?"

"OK."

"Try and get a response from your friend."

I stoked Tyler's pale cheek and spoke her name, but nothing, the silence was deafening.

"No response."

"OK, they aren't far away now."

Seconds later, there was a knock at the front door. I ran down the stairs, unlocked the door, then showed them to where Tyler's limp body was.

I sat back and watched as they stuck things to her body, everything went so slow. They checked her pulse and tried to get a response from her but they couldn't. The last thing I heard before everything went muffled was, "No pulse, we have lost the pulse. Grab the defibrillator."

Tears formed along the rims of my eyes. I let my back fall and hit the wall behind me and watched as my friend lost her battle with life.

The next thing I knew was I stood at the front door with Charles in my arms as Tyler's body lay lifelessly on a stretcher all covered up outside my house.

Everything happened so fast.

"Miss, I'm sorry for your loss, can you think of anything that caused this? Did she have an illness?"

"Not that I'm aware of, she would have told me."

Tyler's body was then slowly put in the back of a black ambulance and that was it. Tyler was gone.

I was left there standing in the dark as I watched the vehicles leave, taking away with them my happiness.

Chapter Five

Buried

Days turned to nights and nights turned to days. The town becoming a ghost of haunted trauma.

Today was the day I dreaded. Two weeks had passed since Tyler's passing. I couldn't help but think back to that awful night. She didn't even die happy; she was in pain, she still grieved the past.

I stood in the hallway barely standing. I looked at my reflection in the mirror. My eyes were dull, I could see my soul had faded by the way I held my shoulders.

Walking into the front room, I just stared blankly at Charles' suit that lay flat across the sofa next to his small body.

I knelt on the floor, reaching out my arms to tuck under Charles' body. Placing him on the floor, I thanked the man in the clouds for giving me a gift that keeps me sane.

I stripped Charles out of his baby grow and then covered up his body with a smart jet-black suit. He looked so handsome, Tyler would have loved this on him, she would have stood there in awe at his cuteness.

Picking Charles up, I made my way to the front door also picking up an envelope filled with pictures of Charles, Tyler and I and a letter that will be buried with her lifeless body this morning.

I opened the front door and made my way to the car. I put Charles in his car seat, doubled checked the pram was in the boot, then got in the driver's seat.

I sat there, my hands gripped the steering wheel. I felt like screaming, but the air was stuck in my lungs. Thoughts raced through the walls of my mind; I was confused. I couldn't believe what had happened. I didn't want to believe that today I would be laying my best friend to rest, the only person whom I developed a loyal friendship with. It scared me at how I watched her smile and laugh, then I watched her die, I watched her life being taken away from her.

I started the engine and took off. The next stop would be the church, where I would walk alongside her coffin. I didn't want to, but her mother insisted. She told me I had bought out the old Tyler, one that's been gone for so long.

It took me an hour until I finally reached the church. As I got closer, you could see the crowd of friends and family stood at the front entrance.

I parked across the road in the car park. I went to the boot, stopping in my tracks remembering that I didn't need his pram because we would be sat down. Whilst I was stood at the back of my car, I reminisced on the memory where I made a joke about Tyler packing up the pram like a professional. The memory made tears escape.

I got Charles out of his seat, placing him swiftly on my hip before making my way over to the crowd of people.

I spotted Tyler's mother, Adele, I rushed straight over to her side.

"Adele," I said, tapping her with my one free hand on her shoulder.

"Olive," she said softly, but evidence of pain flow through her tone of voice.

"How are you? Wait, oh gosh, I'm stupid, sorry that was a stupid question," I babbled, mentally face palming myself.

"Olive, stop rambling, it's OK, I'm fine…how are you?" She said trying to reassure me that I'm not an idiot.

"I'm OK, I guess." Adele hugged me before turning her attention towards Charles.

"How's this little man who looks absolutely adorable in his suit?" Charles wriggled in my arms and let out a tiny giggle as Adele spoke to him.

"Can I hold him?" she questioned.

"Of course." I handed Charles across to Adele's embrace.

Watching Tyler's mother enjoy Charles' company made me happy yet sad. It reminded me of the time Tyler saw Charles. I watched as she embraced him.

After ten minutes, the crowd of people entered the church; whilst Adele, Harrison, Charles and I waited for the coffin in the church's reception area.

This was my first encounter with Harrison. He was a tall, strongly built figure. His eyes were a deep shade of green, his features showed so strongly upon his body, the way his jaw was so pronounced and his smile was so inviting. I could see why Tyler fell instantly for him.

"Hi, I'm Harrison. You must be Olive."

"Hi."

"Tyler spoke about you often, but she never mentioned you have a child?" He looked at me for answers, his deep green eyes piercing through my soul.

"She didn't know until she came here."

"Right, so what's his name?" He reached his hand out to touch Charles.

"Charles," I replied, looking over to see what Adele was doing.

"That's a great name. I always wanted a child with Tyler, but she would always say she wasn't ready." His eyes glistened with sadness.

"I didn't know that, I'm sorry." Something about the impression that Tyler had given me about Harrison started to become a doubt, he seemed genuine but that's on the surface because I knew about Lola. I didn't know him that well after all this is our first interaction.

"Don't worry."

The doors to the church opened and four men came in carrying Tyler's precious soul in that plain wooden box.

Adele wrapped her right arm around my left one, looked at me, took a deep breath, then the music began to play through the door in front of us.

The doors opened and the crowd of people stood up for Tyler's arrival. We began to walk down the aisle. You could see people's tears glistening as they watched Tyler and her memories walk past them.

When we got to the end of the aisle, everyone sat and I took a seat placing Charles on my lap. I watched as Adele took a seat on my left, then Harrison took a seat on my right.

The priest took his position at the stand, leaving the room in complete silence before beginning the ceremony.

"We are gathered here on this day to reminisce and celebrate the life of Tyler James, who unfortunately passed away." To listen to those words stung my heart like a thousand vaults of electricity.

"The family have asked that no questions are to be asked about the cause of death, but to remember Tyler and her life, not to dwell as Tyler would have not have wanted any of you to do so."

The priest held up her memorial card and smiled at the crowd before saying a few words. I looked over at the coffin where Tyler's body lay, but a flashback hit quicker than I could look away.

Flashback

"She isn't responding, check her pulse," the woman double-checked Tyler's pulse whilst the other paramedic checked her airways.

"I can't find anything blocking her airways," the other paramedic said over to the woman.

"She's still not responding, her pulse is very faint." The male paramedic stood up and looked over at Tyler's pale, limp body.

"Is she going to be OK?" I asked walking further into the room, reaching out to hold Tyler's hand.

"I need you to leave the room," the female paramedic said softly to me.

"What? Why?" I protested.

"Sarah, get the defibrillator," he said quickly before pushing me out of the room and closing the door slightly.

"No pulse," the woman yelled.

"1, 2, 3. 1, 2, 3," the man repeated as he tried to regain Tyler's life.

The door opened and the white sheet that once covered Tyler's body protecting her from the world now lay over her body.

"I'm sorry to inform you, but your friend has passed away." Those words forever stuck in my brain like a tattoo.

"No, that's not possible." I cried.

They got the stretcher and called other services to come to collect Tyler. I was too caught up I didn't hear Charles crying. I rushed to grab him then didn't hesitate to follow them outside.

The air was cold, Charles had settled. A black van turned up and parked right next to the ambulance. A tall slim man got out of the van and made his way over to the paramedics.

A paramedic came over to me, he watched me for a while before he spoke up.

"Miss, I'm sorry for your loss. Can you think of anything that may have caused this? Did she have an illness?"

"Not that I'm aware of, she would have told me," I replied.

The ambulance and the van drove off leaving me alone, cold and lost. Tears formed in my eyes, the moon shone down on Charles and me. The empty feeling that had gone now returned to haunt me again.

End of Flashback

"Olive, are you OK?" Adele nudged my arm, I didn't realise that I had blacked out.

"Yeah, sorry," I apologised.

"It's OK, Olive." She placed her hand into my free one gripping it tightly.

"Adele, Tyler's mother would like to say a few words," the priest said. Adele stood up from her seat, gripping in her right hand a crumpled piece of paper that she had written a speech on.

"To Tyler, I never thought this day would come whilst I was still alive, but here I am at my daughter's funeral." Just hearing Adele start with that sentence set the steamy tears flowing down my cheeks.

"I have prepared this speech, scribbled out words and re-wrote this over and over again, but now I don't need it because my words will flow with my heart." Adele crumpled up the piece of paper and slid it into the pocket of her trousers.

"Tyler, where do I start? You were an amazing daughter, who grew into such a strong woman. You had a smile that would light up the room the second you walked into it." Adele began to choke on her tears as she looked around to see the crowd hung on the words about her daughter.

"I remember the day you came into my life and unfortunately, I will never forget the day you left either. Someone once told me that living with memories is a gift and a curse. I now understand what they meant."

The whole church was quiet, a few sniffles escaping here and there. I was trying so hard not to cry. I just sat there listening to Adele's beautiful speech.

"There is one person, whom I would like to thank. She is sat in the front row. Olive, you bought out the life in my child towards the end of her days. Tyler and I would speak over the phone some nights and she would tell me how you showed her life in its different forms. You helped her grow back into her skin. I'm ever so thankful for that and I wish for you to say a few words. I know Tyler would want you too." My body froze. I couldn't believe this.

I panicked, I felt everyone's eyes on me. I didn't know what to do, but I felt I needed to say something as a final goodbye and come to terms with my loss.

I stood up and turned to face the crowd in the room. Adele walked past me, patting my shoulder to give me reassurance that I would do great, but I was still so unsure of what to say.

Adele took Charles off me and sat him on her lap and I walked up and stood beside her coffin, running my fingertips along the edge.

"This came as a big shock to me. I was with Tyler the night of her passing." I began to speak. I took a quick glance over at Adele, who was just simply smiling at me.

"I was there the moment Tyler passed, I would like to try and think that I am lucky that I spent the last hour of Tyler's life by her side, but I'm not because I felt useless."

Tears started falling as I let go of my feelings.

"Tyler and I have been friends since school. We lost contact but recently regained that contact when I bumped into her in a shop." Memories flashed in front of my eyes as I spoke about that day.

"Tyler and I started off where we left off last time, but this time it was slightly different as I have a son now, who was very fond of Tyler, she adored Charles." I looked down at the wide-eyed smiling baby that was sat comfortably on Adele's lap.

"Charles and I will miss Tyler deeply, but she will always remain in our hearts. Charles will always know who Tyler is, I will bring him up to know her as she was. The kind-hearted bubbly bubble of joy." I choked on my words as I spoke and I could see and hear many people do the same as they listened.

"There is so much more I could say, I could stand here for hours on end and talk about Tyler, but time is short and life does go on. I love you, Tyler, don't party too hard without me up there." I stood down, taking one more glance at her coffin before taking my seat in between Harrison and Adele.

"You did amazing," Adele said as she handed Charles back over to me.

"Thank you," I whispered, smiling through my tears.

The priest said some words for Tyler before he began saying some prayers.

"I will ask you all to stand as we sing these hymns," the priest said and everyone stood.

Once the songs had been sung, we all sat back down and had a minute of silence before the service then made its way over to the graveyard.

I heard a sniffle come from beside me and it wasn't Adele. I looked to the right of me to see tears flooding down Harrison's face. I felt sorry for him, even though he's done horrible things, no one deserves to lose someone.

The service in the church ended and everyone made their way to the graveyard, which was only a five-minute walk away.

The rain started to fall from the blanket of grey that was spread across the sky. Everyone stood around the dark hole in the ground. Tyler's coffin lay perfectly next to it.

The priest said meaningful words before her coffin was slowly lowered into the ground. The air filled with heartfelt cries. It was the moment when I truly realised she was never coming back.

Everyone was offered to throw a rose petal into the grave if they wanted to. I took up this offer and walked up to her grave with Adele, Harrison and Charles.

We each threw a rose petal in, Charles sort of dropped his in. We all got to individually stand there for a few seconds, so I took this as my opportunity to throw the envelope full of pictures and a letter into the ground.

"This isn't really goodbye," Adele whispered.

"Bye, Tyler," I whispered through my tears.

"Tyler, I love you and I'm sorry. Take care of our little girl, she needs you more than I do," Harrison broke down. He fell to his knees, he screamed and shouted before resting his head in his hands.

Adele helped him up and took him into a hug. I watched as they cried, feeling myself go. I walked over and joined the hug whilst people carried on saying their goodbyes.

We pulled out of the hug and watched people cherishing Tyler and saying goodbye. I watched someone whom I hadn't seen since that day Tyler passed walked up to her grave, Susan.

"I'm so sorry, Tyler. Goodbye, sweetheart," Susan sobbed before walking over to her car, flashing me a sympathetic smile.

I was shocked she hadn't contacted me or attempted to make any contact since Tyler's passing, I felt angry and upset.

Once the service at the graveyard was over, everyone walked over to the little pub that was just down the road. Walking inside, the owner of the pub had laid out a beautiful buffet across a long table at the back of the pub.

"This is beautiful, thank you, Steve," Adele beamed, hugging the man with all the strength she had left in her.

Adele, Harrison and I took a seat on the table in the corner. I left Charles in his pram; he was sleeping peacefully after the long day we'd both had.

"Do you want a drink?" Harrison asked.

"Yes, please," Adele and I said together.

Harrison got up and walked over to the bar. I watched Adele as she sat closer to me, her face was so pale in this light.

"Harrison is a good kid," Adele said.

"I'm sorry? What are you on about?" I sent Adele a questioning look.

"You know what I mean," she said as Harrison made his way back with the drinks.

I knew exactly what she meant, but her statement confused me. Tyler wouldn't lie to me about anything so serious or does Adele just not see what happens behind closed doors? Deep in thought, I hadn't realised that Harrison had placed the drinks on the table.

"Thank you," I mumbled.

Adele and Harrison started talking between themselves, leaving me to watch as people filled the pub. I watched as Susan walked in, she looked unwell like she carried so much on her shoulders. I decided to go talk to her.

"Susan?" I said, but it came out as more of question. "Olive, how are you?"

"As good as I can get. How are you?"

"I'm fine."

"Why haven't you spoken to me since that night?" I asked, just curious as to why because this was so out of line for Susan.

"I couldn't," she said, hanging her head in shame.

"Why?"

"It reminded me of Ethan, this all reminds me of Ethan."
I felt sorry for her because I guess this is how it went when
Ethan passed away.

"I'm sorry."

"Don't be, this isn't your fault," Susan said softly, smiling
at me.

"I'm going to go over there and talk to some friends. You
know where I am if you need me, Olive." And with that Susan
walked away, leaving me to stand alone.

As I walked back over to my seat, I could hear Charles
crying and I realised that he probably needs feeding.

I arrived back at the table, Adele and Harrison were still
deep in conversation. I picked Charles out of the pram and
placed him against my chest, using my one free arm to reach
into his bag to grab a bottle.

"Do you hand need a hand?" Harrison noticed me
struggling.

"Yes, please." He grabbed the bag that was hooked over
the arm of the pram and placed it on the table.

"No problem. So, how old is this little fella?"

"He's nearly six months old."

"He's got beautiful blue eyes," Harrison said, looking
deeply into Charles' eyes.

"I know." I sat down with Charles on my lap and grabbed
the bottle out of the bag.

It took all of ten minutes to feed Charles. Whilst feeding,
I thought about what Tyler had told me about Harrison, but
what she told me didn't add up to what he was like in person.

"Harrison, if you don't mind me asking, Tyler briefly
mentioned to you." I turned around to face Harrison, who had

now moved across the table to look at something Adele was showing him on her phone.

"She did?" He seemed shocked that she had even mentioned him.

"Yeah, she told me she had a husband called Harrison."

"I'm surprised she even mentioned me."

"Why wouldn't she mention you?" I questioned, eager to know why he would think that.

"That's a long story." He's not getting out of this, I told myself as I pressed on.

"I've got time." He stood up grabbed his empty pint glass and walked right past my chair leaving me stunned by his actions.

I stood up out of the chair and followed him up to the bar. Moving Charles on the other hip so I could get in-between the queue at the bar to get to Harrison.

"Why did you walk away?"

"I needed another drink. Can't you see that my glass is empty?" he smoothly replied.

"What are you so eager to know, Olive?" He said, handing his empty glass to the bartender.

"Nothing." A fake smile plastered across my face.

"That face of yours does not say 'nothing' to me, Olive. You have caution in your eyes." He left me stunned for the second time within minutes.

"Um. Well, maybe we could talk later." I stuttered.

"OK, let's go back to the table," he suggested.

We both sat back down on the chairs at the table and then a small conversation was started. We talked about the memories we shared with Tyler and what a beautiful ceremony was held for her.

Time flew by and before we all knew it, the night sky had rolled in.

I watched Adele, who was stood at the bar ordering another drink. A lot of people started leaving and on their way out, they stood by Adele and wished her all the best. Most of them would say it was such a beautiful day for such a precious girl.

Harrison and I were left alone, we both just sat there in silence. I wished I could use Charles to distract me, but he was fast asleep in his pram and had been for an hour now.

"So, Olive, you were school friends with Tyler, Adele told me?"

"Yeah, we became friends on the first day of secondary school. Did Tyler not mention this?"

"Nope, she just said she knew you from school."

"Oh, OK."

"What is it that you actually wanted to ask me?" Harrison asked, hoping I would let slip easily.

"It's fine, it doesn't really matter now." I nervously laughed.

"OK," he simply replied. I thought he would be cocky about it, I thought he would push for answers.

We sat back in silence again, but this time it was not awkward, it was comfortable.

Adele came back over after seeing a lot of people out. She slouched on the chair with her pint in her hand and sighed heavily, she began to look extremely tired.

"This place shuts in twenty minutes," Adele said, breaking the silence.

"OK," Harrison and I replied in unison.

After about ten minutes, I decided that it would be a good idea to leave. I was getting super tired and Charles was settled.

I got up to leave, but a hand stopped me.

"Olive, thank you for coming today," Adele said, pain showing through the tone of her voice.

"It's not a problem and Adele, I will give you my address so that you can come to visit. I'm sorry though, I'm getting tired and whilst Charles is settled, I would like to take him home." She said nothing back, just nodded and smiled.

I collected all of Charles' bits together, then packed them before making my way out of the pub.

I walked over to my car which was parked just at the end of the street. I unlocked the car and steadily placed Charles in his seat, I didn't want to wake him. I just stood there for a moment admiring how peaceful he looked in his sleep, then a large hand grabbed my shoulder scaring the life out of me.

"Sorry, didn't mean to scare you." I recognised the voice, it was Harrison. *What does he want?* I thought to myself whilst turning around.

"It's OK. What's up?"

"You left without saying goodbye." He seemed hurt by this action.

"I'm sorry," I apologised, feeling somewhat sorry for Harrison.

"Have I done something wrong?" I looked at him in shock. Did he really just ask that question? Anger boiled and I lost it.

"Wrong? Did you do something wrong? You have to be kidding me." I shut the door and yelled at Harrison.

"Olive, I'm so confused. What have I done?" He inched closer to me.

"You used to beat Tyler, you controlled her…you were in the accident that killed your child because you wanted to spend time with your child because you hadn't spent time with her because you were out cheating on Tyler," I yelled pushing him away with my hands firmly, tears now spilling down my face.

"Olive, what are you on about?"

"You know what I'm on about," I said, anger evident through the harsh tone in my voice.

"Olive, you have got this all wrong. I've been working away for four months. I got offered a job after Lola's death. Tyler and I agreed we needed our space after it because Lola's death had taken a toll on our marriage." He grabbed my arms, lifting my head to face him.

"That's not true, it can't be. Tyler would never lie to me." I stuttered, nothing he would say would make me believe him.

"Olive you have to believe me. I know you have only just met me, but there is so much that needs to be said." I just stood there staring at Harrison.

"This is too much," I said, turning around and opened the driver's side door.

"Olive, wait, here's my number. Please just give me a chance to explain." He slipped a piece of paper into my hand and walked away.

I watched as his silhouette walked down the dimly lit street back into the pub. I sat in the car and just let the thoughts and memories of the day consume me.

I finally started the car and made my way home.

It felt so quick on the way home because I arrived at my front door in the blink of an eye.

"Come on then, Charles, let's get you to bed."

I picked Charles' tiny body out of his car seat and lay him upon my chest. His little head relaxed against my shoulder.

Unlocking the front door, I slowly walked in making sure that my upper body didn't make too much movement to wake Charles up.

The house was dark and the air that surrounded our bodies was cold. You could tell the winter months were coming fast.

I turned the upstairs lights on, it illuminated the way to my bedroom. Opening my bedroom door, I looked to my right where my bed looked so inviting after this eventful day.

Before I could climb into that comfortable bed, I had to place my little angel into his bed. Laying his fragile body into the baby blue blanket, I saw his features. I had been so caught up in all that had happened and all that had been going on, I hadn't noticed how he had grown into his skin; his features had become more pronounced.

I stood there for ages star gazing at my beautiful creation. My eyes became sore as my eyelids dropped further and further over my eyes. I took this as a sign to climb into my own cloud of comfort. Letting my head sink into the pillows, I took one last long breath in before drifting off to sleep.

I was awoken by the vibration of my phone, rattling away on the wooden top of my bedside table. I lifted my head out from between the sheets and the pillows. Letting my eyes adjust to my surroundings, I then picked up the phone.

"Hello?" Tiredness showing in my voice as I croaked.

The line was dead quiet on the other end.

"Hello, who's this?" Nothing.

"Excuse me? Hello? Anyone there?" I began to become frustrated. I wiped my phone screen to see that it was only four-thirty in the morning. Who would be calling me at this time?

"Why the hell are you calling me at this time whoever you are?" Anger was definitely evident in my voice. I heard shuffling from the other end of the line but no words.

"Bye." I hung up, completely annoyed that someone could be so inconsiderate.

Lazily letting my head flop back onto the pillows, I closed my eyes but struggled to get back to sleep.

I just lay there, every now and then picking up my phone to check the time. I stared at the ceiling and just let my body relax.

After what felt like hours, my eyes finally closed and I went back to sleep.

Chapter Six

From Lost to Love

I opened my eyes, blinking a few times to re-adjust to the sunlight that filtered through the curtains lighting up the room.

I picked up my phone to see what time it was. I was shocked to see it was only eight-thirty in the morning. I took the opportunity whilst Charles was still sound asleep to just relax in my own company.

I looked over towards the window where the rays of sun broke through the fabric of the curtains. I sat up and placed my bare feet on the carpet.

I stood up and opened the curtains letting the light blind me. Sighing heavily, I took in the views, the sky was so clear, I could see the waves crashing into the golden sands.

I opened the window and listened to the sounds of nature. You could hear the wind blowing through the open sky and the birds singing.

My silent time was disturbed by the vibration of my phone. I walked over and picked it off the nightstand and answered the call.

"Hello? Look, if this is the same person that called me at early hours of this morning, then please leave," I said, feeling slightly annoyed.

"Hello, OK, that's it, I'm going to hang up."

"Wait," a voice interrupted me.

"Harrison?" I raised my eyebrows.

"Yeah, sorry about that. I called you last night, but I didn't know what to say if I'm honest. Sorry if I annoyed you." He did sound apologetic.

"It's fine, I guess. Why are you calling me anyway? And how did you get my number?" I questioned.

"Adele gave me your number. I just had this feeling you would never call me and I think we need to talk."

"Talk about what?" I sounded sarcastic.

"Don't play dumb, Olive. There is more than meets the eye and I do believe you wanted to ask me something, your eyes said it all last night." He was so straight forward.

"Yeah OK, fine. When and where do you want to meet?"

"Do you have anywhere in mind, somewhere where we can talk? Preferably away from the public eye, more private."

"Yeah, I will message Adele to see if she can have Charles." I sighed, really not wanting to do this, especially after all the drama that's been non-stop.

"Perfect, so where are we meeting?"

"I will send you my address. See you at about 2 o'clock?"

"OK," was the last thing I heard before the call ended.

I just stood staring at my phone, trying to process everything. I think it's fair to say that over the last few weeks, I've been overwhelmed with events and now my brain and body are tired.

Charles began to muffle baby sounds. I instantly walked over to his cot and took him out.

I sat at the end of my bed with Charles laying on my lap. I don't know what came over me when Harrison asked to meet and talk. I guess there was a part of me that wanted to know the truth.

I hadn't realised how long that I'd been sat at the end of my bed until I received a message on my phone. I picked my phone up from under my leg and saw the message was from Harrison.

The message read, "Hey, it's Harrison. I was wondering if we could meet earlier?" I sighed remembering that I hadn't even called Adele to have Charles.

I stood up, Charles still laying perfectly in my arms. I decided on not wasting any more time getting lost in thoughts.

I opened a chest of draws that was next to Charles' cot and picked out a dark pair of jeans with a white jumper.

Laying Charles on the bed, I decided to get him dressed first. First, I put on the white jumper, then the blue jeans, he looked so cute and innocent.

I decided that I would wear something similar to what I had dressed Charles in. So, I went over to my wardrobe and grabbed an off-white t-shirt and some light blue ripped skinny jeans.

After I had gotten the both of us dressed, I made my way into the kitchen, placed Charles on his play mat in the front room, then prepared him a bottle and some food.

As I walked into the front room to give Charles his bottle, I remembered that I hadn't messaged Harrison back about meeting earlier.

I quickly fed Charles his bottle, then switched the TV on a baby channel before running upstairs and grabbing my phone off the edge of the bed.

I read over the screen to see that I had three missed calls from Harrison and multiple messages.

'From Harrison: Olive, can I come around now?'

'From Harrison: Olive?'

'From Harrison: Hello, are you there?'

'From Harrison: Olive, are you ignoring me? I'm sorry for annoying you with the phone calls this morning'

'3 Missed calls: From Harrison'

I sighed. Why was he so desperate to meet me and talk? Plus, I'm the one who wants to question him. Surely, he's not that excited. I unlocked my phone and began to type a reply when there was a knock at the front door. I rushed back downstairs and opened the door.

"Hey." It was Harrison, who looked worried.

"Hi. Are you OK?" I asked slightly concerned.

"Yeah. I got worried when you didn't answer your phone."

"I'm fine, I was just busy, sorry. Come in." I moved aside so he could enter.

I lead Harrison into the front room, where Charles still lay on his play mat. The blue-eyed baby looked over at Harrison smiling.

"Take a seat." I pointed at the grey sofa.

"Thanks," he said as he sat firmly down on the sofa.

"Harrison, why did you need to see me earlier?" I asked because his behaviour was weird.

"I…Um…Well, I don't actually know. I just felt the need to come and see you as soon as I could," he rambled on.

"OK, well, I can call Adele and ask her now if she will have Charles. In all honesty, I forgot to call her." I grabbed my phone, but before I could find Adele's number, Harrison spoke up.

"No, it's OK, I mean that's if you don't want Charles to be here, I saw a beach, maybe we could take him for a walk?" I hadn't a clue where any of this was coming from, but I didn't want to spend another day away from Charles.

"OK, that would be nice. I guess Charles and I haven't left the house since Tyler's passing." Just the thought of that memory bought back steamy tears into the rims of my eyes.

"That sounds like a plan. Shall we head for our walk now, only because the weather isn't so good later?" he said sensing the sadness.

"Yeah, sure I just need to get the pram out of the car." I stood up and I was just about to walk out of the front room, but I felt a tight grip on my arm and it startled me.

"Sorry, I didn't mean to scare you. I can get the pram from the car if you want?" I admit I felt slightly scared, but I think it was because of what Tyler had told me.

"Yeah, OK, thank you," I mumbled, he just shot me a smile before leaving the front room, then seconds later, I heard the front door open.

I picked Charles off his play mat and held him tightly to my chest, then walked towards the front door.

As I walked out the front door, I could see Harrison setting up the pram for Charles. The closer I got to him, I couldn't tell whether the nerves I was feeling were because I was scared of him or because I was scared of finding out something else that would throw my mind into a frenzy.

"Let's go then," Harrison said as I made sure Charles was all snuggled up in his pram.

We walked for about twenty minutes in pure silence. It wasn't until Harrison stopped for no reason that a conversation started.

"Olive, what did you want to talk about?" I gulped knowing that he wasn't going to forget about it.

"Well, I mean it's nothing important," I stated, but I could tell by the way he turned to me and raised his eyebrows that he knew I was lying.

"Olive, I know you're lying. I can see it in your eyes." He laughed.

"It's not something that you can just come out with," I said quite rudely. I don't know why I said it like that but Harrison fell silent. I felt bad for snapping at him, but just let the silence eat away at us again.

We had walked right down towards the edge of the water, the water glistening every now and then, as the sun broke through the clouds.

The silence was so cold that you could hear the wind floating around us, whistling past our ears.

I just watched as Harrison stood beside me, his features looked like heaven. His eyes were glued on the view ahead. His beauty was so pure, his pale powder-white skin so smooth and the way his jaw was so pronounced.

"Are you staring at me?" I didn't even realise how long I had been staring at him until he spoke up. A blush crept its way onto my pale cheeks giving the game away.

"No." He just looked at me, his eyes looking right into mine.

"Really?" He smirked.

"OK, fine, maybe I was, but why does it matter?" I fired back, I was completely and utterly embarrassed.

"Don't be embarrassed. I've been taking in your beautiful complexion since the first day I laid eyes on you." Butterflies erupted in my stomach, but it felt so wrong to hear him say these words, so close to having lost Tyler, he was her's.

"You can't say that."

"Why, because of Tyler? You don't know the half of it." When he said those words, you could hear the anger inside him. It was like something just snapped at the mention of her name. Was he grieving?

"I'm sorry," I said, feeling guilty.

We walked yet again in silence, but this time it was awkward and uncomfortable. We walked along the edge of the water for a good ten minutes before one of us finally spoke up.

"I'm sorry," we said at the same time, we both broke out into fits of laughter.

"I didn't mean to snap at you back there. It's just I'm sick of people thinking I'm the bad guy." You could hear the drop of annoyance in his tone of voice, you could see he was genuinely fed up.

"I don't think you're a bad person," I spluttered out.

"Don't lie to me, Olive. I can see you're scared of me, by the way, you flinched when I grabbed your arm and the way your eyes dart away from mine." As he said those words, I actually felt sorry for him because he was right.

Why am I lying? I shouldn't be lying.

"I know, I'm sorry. I think we should go and have that chat now," I said softly.

"Shall we go back then? It's getting cold." Harrison said, rubbing his purple hands together.

"Yeah, I was just about to say, let's go back, then we can get in the warm and talk."

We both smiled at each other before walking back up the beach feeling satisfied.

It took all of twenty minutes to walk up the damp sandy beach before we arrived at the face of my front door.

"After you," Harrison said before gently brushing his hand over the small of my back.

"Thank you, such a gentleman." I sniggered as I pushed the pram into the open hallway.

Harrison followed behind me pushing my front door shut. I picked Charles up and laid him across my chest in the hope that he would settle and fall asleep.

Harrison and I both took a seat on the sofa and I placed Charles behind me so he couldn't wriggle off.

"So?" he said.

"So?" I giggled.

"What did you want to talk about?" His facial expression changed through emotions. I couldn't tell what he was thinking.

"Well, Tyler and I, we had a conversation about you," I said the last part of the sentence quietly.

"What did you talk about?" he pressed on.

"Well, Tyler was not herself, then one-night long story short, she told me about you, how you two met then what you did." I sort of rushed out every word as I spoke.

"What I did?" He sent me a questioning look.

"Yeah, like the whole working late and the abuse and Lola," I said more like a question.

"Working late? Abuse? Lola? What did she say about Lola?" His eyes darted around with so many questions.

"She said you were driving the car when it crashed." I looked up at Harrison, whose face fell at the mention of his daughter's name.

"She said I was driving?" He almost choked out.

"Yes, weren't you?" I could see the tears slip over the rims of his eyes.

"No."

"Well, who was?."

"Tyler," he almost whispered. I honestly didn't know at this point whether to believe him or not.

"What?"

"Tyler."

"No, I heard what you said, I just don't get why she would lie. I mean that's if you're telling the truth."

"That's what she did best, lie." It hurt to hear Harrison say that about Tyler, but before I could call him liar, he pulled out his phone and handed it to me.

My eyes scanned over the newspaper article that was on the phone screen. It read, '*Mothers Who Speed Kill.*' My breath hitched.

'Mother, Tyler James, twenty-two years of age crashed into a tree. Most of the car was folded. The mother of Lola James survived, unfortunately, one-year-old Lola James was deceased before medical help could reach her.' By the time I had read the last few words the tears were already streaming down my cheeks like a fire burning my skin.

'Tyler James was known to have been driving above the speed limit, the weather conditions made it difficult to drive.'

I took a quick glance to see Harrison, his face dripping with tears like mine.

'Tyler James received a prison sentence of four months and a £700 fine. This mother has lost her child, that is her sentence, she will have to live with the guilt.' I read over some comments before deciding that I had seen enough and I handed the phone back to Harrison.

"Harrison."

"Don't be sorry." He wiped the remaining tears from under his eyes.

"Carry on, what else did she say?"

"Well, she said you worked away a lot, she thought you may have been cheating on her, but now I've seen what I have just seen, I'm doubting everything she ever told me," I said honestly.

"Olive, you can believe some things she's told you. Tyler was just very unstable and the medication she was put on made her worse."

"I don't know. I'm just trying to figure out things. I've been lied to a lot lately," I confessed.

"I'm not going to lie to you. I don't even know you," he said, making me realise that he didn't know me so why would he lie to me. He gave me the evidence.

"OK, but what about those late nights and the whole cheating thing."

"Right, I will own up to this. It was after Lola had passed and Tyler couldn't cope anymore. She kept blaming me, then blaming herself. I tried to talk to her, but she just ignored me day in and day out." Guilt spread over his entire body and he tensed up to what he was about to say next.

"OK." I sensed that he had become tense, so I placed my hand on his knee.

"I used to get drunk. I would go to the pub just to be away from home. I hated being in that house, it was deadly quiet without hearing Lola's screams every five seconds."

He paused before rubbing his sweaty hands on his jeans.

"I saw this girl at the bar, she saw me and we got talking. She made me feel wanted. Tyler and I were so young when we fell in love and Lola's death was the last straw before the breaking point. We argued a lot over little things, but it wasn't healthy. Then Tyler fell pregnant and we became strong again because of Lola." He was rushing his words out like he wanted to get straight to the point.

"Lola was the only thing that held us together. I do feel so guilty about Tyler and me, what I did with that girl. I shouldn't have done it; I know that now. I told Tyler we needed a break, so she came back here and I stayed home because of work. So, yes, I did cheat on her, she knows I did, I told her." He hates himself for his actions and I could see that in his eyes.

"What about the abuse?"

"Abuse?" He looked shocked and hurt that Tyler would ever say such a thing.

"She said you abused her and she had bruises on her arm too."

"I would never lay a finger on her. She went through a stage of hurting herself. In the mornings, I would wake up and she would have beaten herself black and blue. It killed me seeing her like that, that's why I told her to go home. Adele was supposed to be coming down with me when she came back from holiday, which would have been this week."

"Wait, so you and Adele were coming here this week to see Tyler?"

"Yeah, that Susan woman, we saw her at Ethan's funeral."

"That all adds up now." My mind slowly working out the events in order.

"Did you ever meet Ethan?" I asked out of curiosity.

"No, Tyler and I never came back to her home town. I just heard a lot about him, you and his wife, Jessica, I think that's her name." I cringed at the sound of her name and Harrison sensed my mood change since hearing her name.

"Do you not like Jessica?" he asked, a slight smirk playing at the corners of his lips.

"I wouldn't say I don't like her; I just am not so keen on her."

"Why would that be?" I could tell Harrison was enjoying this.

"She was just overpowering as a person. Friendly but too friendly for my liking. She was too innocent like she was really good at lying."

"So, she acted so innocently, but she was disguised as the devil."

"Yes." We both sat there and laughed before we were interrupted by Charles crying. I stood up and placed Charles back on my chest, his head resting lightly on my shoulder.

"I will be back in a minute, just going to put him to bed as it's getting late." Harrison nodded in reply.

I walked out of the front room and up the same old staircase that I could probably walk blindfolded now.

I finally got to my bedroom door, slowly pushed it open not wanting to disturb Charles as he settled quickly between the space of me picking him up to enter the bedroom.

I lay his little body in the cot, covering him with a soft cotton blanket and tucking it under his sides. I stood there and stared at the precious baby before making my way out of the bedroom and back downstairs.

"Well, that didn't take you long," Harrison said as I slumped back on the sofa.

"It never does, he's an easy sleeper." I sighed heavily.

"Is that his dad?" Harrison said, standing up and pointing to a picture of Ethan and me.

"Yes, there's no point in lying to you." I stood up and joined Harrison in front of the picture.

"Who is that? I recognise his face." Harrison said, turning to face me. I let my smile fall.

"That's Ethan." Harrison sensed that I had become upset because he embraced me in a hug.

"I thought you two where just friends, I didn't realise. I'm sorry." His words were muffled due to his mouth being blocked by my hair.

"It's fine a lot of people know now, I kept it quiet at first."

"That's understandable." He grabbed his hands in mine, rubbing his thumbs over my forehands.

Feelings sparked inside of me, just the touch of his skin on mine made me feel wanted and loved. Even if he was a complete stranger.

"Do you want to talk about it?"

"No, not right now. I just want to forget everything that's happened," I said removing myself from his grip.

"That's fine, maybe if you want to, we could watch some films. I don't mind going to the shop and getting some nibbles."

"Yeah, OK. That would be nice as long as you don't mind going to the shop. If you don't want to, I can go."

"No, I will go, you have a sleeping child upstairs." Harrison laughed, reminding me about Charles.

"Yeah, good idea, you get the nibbles. I will find a film to watch."

Harrison smiled at me before taking his car keys out of his pocket. I checked the time on my phone to see that it was only 8 o'clock.

I walked Harrison to the front door and suggested the best shop to go to. Then I watched him get in his car and drive off.

I walked back in the front room and for the first time in months my mind wasn't confused and I wasn't thinking about all the negative things that had been and gone. I was actually thinking about Harrison; I couldn't get him out of my mind.

Harrison came back about forty minutes later. I forgot how long it would take to go into town and then back. All the time Harrison was gone, I struggled to keep myself awake.

He hung his coat up on the railing of the staircase before joining me on the sofa, his cheeks burn bright red from the cold.

The light from the TV lit up our faces as we started to watch a movie. We took a moment whilst the introduction of the movie played to send each other a soft smile.

As the film neared the end. I hadn't realised how close we had gotten. Our hands lay next to each other, nearly touching.

I don't think Harrison noticed the distance between our bodies because he was glued to the screen, so before he could notice, I moved away slowly.

The film credits started rolling down the TV and Harrison let a yawn escape his lips.

"Been a long day," he said as I turned off the TV and switched on the side lamp.

"It sure has, it's getting pretty late," I stated.

"Yeah, I should probably get going." He stood up and patted down his jeans.

"Yeah, I will show you out, then I'm going to hit the pillow and instantly fall asleep." I laughed quietly.

We both walked out of the front room. Harrison followed behind me and grabbed his coat before I opened the front door.

The cold air of the night hit me as soon as it opened causing a shiver to erupt down my spine.

"Guess I will see you again sometime," Harrison said as his body brushed against mine when he walked past me to go to his car.

"Yeah, see you around."

I watched as he jumped in his car. He sent me a small smile making my stomach do backflips.

His car drove away, his headlights disappearing into the black of the night. I walked back inside and locked the front door before smiling to myself and making my way to bed.

I laid in bed. I thought that because I was so tired and with it being late, I would just fall straight to sleep, but I was wrong.

My mind filtered with thoughts about Harrison, the way he comforted me even though he was hurting too. His eyes where so beautiful, they could look right past everything.

I turned over trying not to think about Harrison. I didn't want to become attached, to get hurt. I didn't want any more broken promises.

The harder I tried to erase him, the more I thought about him. I was fighting a losing battle with my mind. I gave in and fell asleep dreaming of his smile.

I woke up feeling fresh and ready for the day. I decided that I was going to take Charles to town, he needed some new clothes as he was starting to grow a little more every day.

I got out of bed and changed into some clothes that had just been dumped at the back of my wardrobe. I never thought I looked pretty in them, but something inside me changed.

I stepped into these light blue jeans that had rips just under the knees, then I placed on this off the shoulder white jumper. I glanced at my appearance in the mirror extremely satisfied with myself.

Then after I had stared at myself for a good few minutes, I grabbed Charles a smart navy tracksuit and placed it on him. I wasted no time in preparing Charles' feed before strapping him into his car seat then started the drive to town.

I reached the small town after twenty minutes of driving. I pulled into the local car park just to the side of town, but I was struggling to find a parking space.

Once I had parked the car, I went straight to the boot and grabbed Charles' pram. Then I put it as close to Charles' door as I could get it.

After finally getting Charles in his pram, I headed off down the street, many shops came into view. I decided on going into the first shop I saw that simply had beautiful clothes hanging from mannequins. Walking into the shop, the range of fabrics filled my eyesight.

About two hours later, I became fed up of going in and out of shops, there is only so much you can look at. I made my way out of the shop and walked over to the road towards the end of town.

I found a little cafe. I walked in the smell of freshly baked cakes hit my nostrils. My mouth instantly watered.

Sitting down at a table at the back of the cafe, I looked over the menu to see what they had to eat. Whilst deciding what to have I heard movement across the table. I peered over the top of the menu to see Harrison staring at me in amusement.

"Are you stalking me, Olive?" I raised my eyebrow at his attempt to make me laugh.

"No, are you stalking me?" He just laughed before picking up the other menu.

"Yes, as long as you don't mind." His eyes darted around the menu as he contemplated what to have.

Minutes later, Harrison and I decided what we wanted to eat and ordered.

"What brought you to town?" Harrison said, making direct eye contact with me.

"Just to get out of the house. You?" I asked as the waitress bought over our drinks.

"Pretty much the same as you." He took a sip from his tea, pulling a face as he burnt his tongue.

"Hot?" I laughed.

"Yeah. That wasn't funny," he said dead serious.

"Ouch." I laughed harder, placing my hands on my sides.

We sat there and both laughed at Harrison's stupidity and it didn't take long after that, our food was bought out and boy did it smell good.

"How's your food?" Harrison said trying to make conversation.

"My food is great, thanks. What about yours?"

"It's amazing," he said with a mouth full of food.

Both of us where in fits of laughter again until I watched Harrison's expressions change, he went as white as a ghost.

I looked at him, concerned. He just smiled at me, but I could tell something wasn't right.

"Are you OK?"

"Yeah, I'm fine, don't worry, I thought I saw...Never mind." He shook his head.

"Tyler?"

"Erm, yeah." He bowed his head down in shame.

"That's OK. I thought I saw Ethan all the time after he passed."

Harrison remained quiet, so I just shut up and let him grieve in his own way.

The rest of the time we had spent eating was in pure silence and it was awkward.

Once we had both finished our food, we just stared at each other before Harrison spoke up breaking the ice.

"I'm sorry."

"Don't be, you have been through a lot, we both have."

I grabbed his hand and a flame ignited inside of me.

"Do you want to come around again?" I blurted out.

"Yeah, sure." Harrison stood up and walked over to the cashier. I looked at him sending him daggers, he was not about to pay for this. I jumped off my seat and ran over grabbing my card from my coat pocket, but I was too late.

"Why did you pay for it?" I groaned.

"Because I'm a gentleman." He laughed, placing his hand on my back.

"Yeah, right," I joked back as we headed back to the table to collect our things.

Harrison grabbed Charles' pram from my grip and began to push it out of the cafe. The feeling of guilt dropped over my shoulders. It should be Ethan doing that.

He must have sensed that my mood had changed because he slung his arm over my shoulder making all the thoughts go away.

We finally got back to the car after Harrison decided that he would point out the B&B he was staying at. I couldn't believe it was right in the middle of town.

Harrison placed the pram in the boot whilst I put Charles in the car. Once we were all settled, I started the drive back to my house.

We were about halfway home when Harrison decided he was going to speak his thoughts aloud.

"What are we?" It took me by shock, this is not how I imagined this conversation.

"Excuse me?" I stuttered.

"Don't get me wrong. I still love Tyler, but I can't get you out of my mind. Things happen for a reason. Like Tyler's death brought us together…I feel like I have known you for years." He rambled on.

"Well, I do feel the same, but it's just wrong." I shook my head, suddenly not wanting to talk about this.

"We can't ignore how we feel, Olive."

"I know because I've been non-stop thinking about you since my eyes first met yours." I took a deep breath after realising that I had let my feelings speak for me.

"This is going to sound crazy, but, Olive, can we try?"

"Try what?" I gulped, knowing exactly when he meant.

"Don't play stupid with me now, this is not the time." He nervously laughed.

"Yes." Yet again, I let my feelings speak for me.

It felt amazing to let my feelings go, but a part of me didn't know whether this was right, it felt right but so wrong.

As soon as he heard those words, his smile spread from ear to ear and I relaxed letting an actual smile appear on my face.

We sat in comfortable silence all the way back to my house. It felt so weird that only a few days ago, Harrison was just a stranger with a dangerous past, but now he was someone I came to trust.

The drive home came to a halt as we had reached the destination. I walked up to the front door and unlocked it.

I turned around to go back and get Charles out of the car, but when I looked, Harrison cradled his body and walked into the house. I stood there and smiled like an idiot. I walked in, shut the door and then started a new chapter in my life.

Chapter Seven
Time Flies

The months had flown by and Harrison had moved in with Charles and me about a month ago.

Things couldn't be any better. Charles' birthday was coming up in the next few days and there had been no more drama since Harrison and I spoke after Tyler's funeral.

Today, I woke up next to the usual warmth of Harrison's body. I just lay there and stared at his complexion and thought to myself how had I become so lucky to find Harrison.

It had me thinking that maybe people are right. When at my darkest times, they say to me everything happens for a reason.

Whilst I was lost in thought, I had missed the fact that Harrison was awake and staring back at me.

"What are you thinking about?" The huskiness of his voice rattling as he spoke.

"Nothing."

"I know that face, Olive, we have been together long enough for me to know what that face means." He sat up and pulled me into his chest.

"Just thinking about the phrase, everything happens for a reason," I said pulling away and looking deep into his eyes.

"It means—" He started before I cut him off.

"I know what it means." I laughed.

"Then what about it?" he questioned.

"Well, if Tyler hadn't died, I would have never met you and if I had never gone to town that day with Charles, I would have never have found Tyler." I sighed realising that there are good and bad vibes about these memories.

"Stop worrying about the past and live in the moment. Memories are different, you need to remember the good ones and eliminate the bad. Then you will be able to have a clear mind," Harrison said whilst moving out of bed and heading over to the cupboard.

"I know, it's just sometimes, the good memories come along with the bad." I heard Harrison sigh because he hated that I had an answer for everything.

I got out of bed myself, walked up behind Harrison and hugged him.

"Thank you," I whispered before releasing his body from my embrace and walking out of the bedroom.

I walked across the hallway to what was once the spare room, but it was now Charles' room. Harrison and I decided about a little over two months ago to try put him in his own room. So far, Charles has slept soundly in his room, but a part of me wishes Harrison had finished decorating the room before we decided to move Charles in there.

I walked into the room that had half painted walls and spotted a little body in the cot. His chest was rising up and down. I stood leaning against the wall over Charles cot, his eyes were still shut, he looked peaceful. I was stuck in a trance of my son's beauty that I didn't realise Harrison was stood next to me also taking in the wonderful sight.

"You have done a great job," he said and wrapped his arms around my waist whilst resting his head on my shoulder.

"You tell me every day." I turned and smiled, but just before I went to connect our lips, a smiley eyed baby looked right through the bars and giggles.

"Well, I shall go make us all some breakfast. You two get ready," Harrison said as he walked out of the room.

I walked over to the set of draws where all of Charles' clothes were kept and opened the bottom draw. As soon as I opened it, I instantly found the outfit that I would dress him in.

I placed Charles on the changing table that Harrison had bought him as a thanking gift for me letting him live with Charles and me.

"Right, Charles, let's get you dressed."

I pulled a yellow t-shirt over his head before placing a pair of dark navy jeans over his tiny legs. I decided on trying to put a pair of soft-bottom shoes on his feet as I know it wouldn't be long until he would be walking.

After I had dressed Charles and myself, I walked downstairs placing Charles on the floor in the living room. Then I let my nose follow the scent of bacon, which led me to the kitchen.

"Something smells good." I always complemented Harrison's cooking because he never failed to impress me.

"Breakfast is served." He laid two plates full of an English breakfast on the table in front of me; whilst grabbing a small plastic bowl with chopped up pieces of bacon, beans and sausage at the side of the table. Then I watched him as he left the kitchen and came back with Charles putting him in his high chair.

"Thank you." I muffled as I said with a mouth full of food.

"No need to thank me, it's the least I can do." He smiled weakly.

We sat eating in silence with Charles talking baby every few seconds.

"Olive, I have to go somewhere today to sort out some stuff for work. Do you think you could ask Adele or Susan over to help you with preparations for Charles' birthday tomorrow?" Harrison placed his knife and fork down on the table.

"Yeah, I mean I guess. Is this work thing really that important, can't it wait till Monday?" I questioned even though I knew the answer already.

"I'm sorry, but it's important. I will make it up to you."

I just nodded in response and watched as Harrison got up from his place at the table and put his dirty plate in the dishwasher.

"I will be back after." That was the last thing I heard as Harrison walked out of the front door leaving Charles and me for the third time this week.

I just picked at my food, not really wanting it. Over the last few weeks, Harrison had been so distracted, he has this look on his face, pretty much twenty-four-seven and I have seen this face before I know I have but I can't remember where.

Charles began to become fussy with his food, so I took this as an opportunity to get these thoughts out of my mind.

I picked up the baby fork that lay alongside Charles' bowl and stabbed a piece of bacon.

"Open wide," I said, making the action with my own mouth, followed by the noise, "Ahh." As I pushed the fork closer to Charles' mouth, he opened his mouth taking in the food.

"Good boy."

After helping Charles eat his food, I decided to clean up the kitchen because after Harrison cooks, it always looks like a bomb has hit it.

Once the kitchen was cleaned, I put Charles back on the living room floor and went upstairs to get my phone off the nightstand to call Susan.

"Hello?"

"Hi, Susan, it's Olive."

"Hello, love. Everything all right?"

"Yeah, I was wondering if you could come over and help me with some things for Charles' birthday tomorrow." I nibbled the ends of my nails waiting for a reply.

"Of course. When should I come round?"

"Now, I mean that's only if you want to come right now."

"I will be there in about thirty minutes."

"OK. Thank you, I'm just going to call Adele too."

"OK, love, see you soon."

After ending the call to Susan, I scrolled down my contact list and found Adele's number and pressed call.

I let the phone ring for a good five minutes but nothing. I kept trying, but maybe she was busy. I laid my phone on the arm of the sofa and began to clean the hallway.

About ten minutes later, I heard my phone going off in the living room. I dumped the hoover against the side of the stairs and grabbed my phone to see that Adele was calling me back.

"Hello," I said, sounding completely out of breath.

"Hi, Olive. Is everything OK?"

"Yeah, I was just going to ask if you could come round and help prepare for Charles' birthday tomorrow. Susan is coming too."

"Why isn't Harrison helping you?" She sounded confused.

"He has this work thing he needs to sort out. He's been out for most of the week."

"OK, I will be there within the next hour."

"Thank you, see you soon."

I ended the call and plopped myself down on the sofa and decided that I would just wait and tidy things when Susan arrived.

I sat on the sofa, letting my head fall back. I let my thoughts consume me. I started thinking about the time that Harrison confessed he'd had an affair with Tyler.

It led me to think about whom he had an affair with. Was she pretty, was she everything I'm not?

My thoughts were interrupted by a knock at the door. I got up and made my way over to the front door to see a cold Susan.

I opened the door and we embraced each other in a hug.

"I feel like I haven't seen you in years," Susan beamed.

"It has been a long time, a few months," I said leading her into the front room, where I offered to hang her coat up.

"How have you been?" Susan said softly whilst picking Charles up off the floor.

"Yeah, we have been good, I just can't believe my little baby is one tomorrow."

"Time flies, you should know that. Your mum used to tell you all the time." I laughed because I knew my mum used to literally tell me every night before I went to sleep.

"How have you been, Susan?" I sat down next to her.

"I have been well, thank you. Why isn't Harrison helping you?" she asked, questioning me like she was my mum.

"He's been dealing with some work stuff, he said it's important," I replied, knowing exactly what words would fall from her mouth next.

"I have a bad feeling about him. I don't like him, only for your sake will I be civil." I just sent her a small smile.

"You sound like my mum." I laughed.

"You know she wanted me to look after you." I just nodded because I knew my mum would want Susan out of all the people to look after me, my mum trusted Susan with her life.

"Want to get started?" I could tell Susan felt awkward about Harrison and so I played it off.

"Yeah, sure. Let's go," I said.

"We can start by making the cake, just leave him on the floor he can play with his toys." I watched as Susan placed him on the floor and then she followed me out into the kitchen.

Susan and I laid the ingredients across the worktops and we were about to begin when there was a knock at the door.

I looked at Susan who simply waved her hand in the air ushering me to go answer the door whilst she started on the cake.

I opened the door to see Adele.

"Hi," I said, letting her walk past me. Adele took off her shoes and hung her coat up, then walked straight into the living room.

"Oh, Adele, we are in the kitchen making the cake." I peeked my head around the corner of the living room door to see her already holding Charles in her arms.

"It's OK, I will stay here and look after Charles."

"He's fine in here, Adele." I looked over at her and she placed Charles back on the floor and made her way into the kitchen.

"Right, OK, Susan if you bake the base of the cake. Adele, do you mind helping me wrap some presents?"

"Yeah, sure," Adele replied.

Adele and I went to the far end of the kitchen and began to wrap presents that I had bought over the last few months.

I knew that Susan was happy doing the cake. I remember back when I was younger, my mum and Susan would make amazing cakes for Ethan and me. I smiled at these happy memories, knowing that time has replayed itself as I have grown older.

"Olive, how are you and Harrison?" Adele asked as she grabbed the sellotape that hung on the edge on the wooden table.

"We are good." I smiled weakly, having this feeling curdle in my stomach.

"You sure?" I raised my eyebrow. I thought to myself for a second before answering.

"Yeah, we are fine."

"Why isn't he here? I thought this was his week off?" My smile dropped knowing she had spoken to him and he didn't even tell me.

"He got called in today and yes, he had but there is a lot of problems going on at his work I think." I gritted my teeth as I let the words fall freely.

"You aren't happy about that, are you?" Adele had now stopped wrapping presents and her eyes are darting right at me.

"Well, no, not really."

"Why don't you tell him?"

"I have once or twice, but he tells me he will make it up to me and I guess I'm the one who falls for it." I bitterly laughed as I realised how over the last few months. I have been so gullible.

"You need to be firm with him."

"I know." I sighed, feeling defeated by Adele's words.

Silence settled between us, we both carried on wrapping presents.

"What do you think?" Susan's voice echoed down the far end of the kitchen.

I walked over to Susan and saw that the worktops were now covered in flour and eggshells.

"I have got a design in mind," Susan said pulling a piece of paper across the unit.

"When did you design this?" I stood in awe over the effort and detail for Charles' cake.

"Pretty much all day yesterday," she said proudly.

"How did you know I was going to ask you to do the cake," I questioned not really knowing how she knew I would ask her to do the cake.

"I had a hunch; you always loved my baking as a child."

Susan knew me too well and I loved her to bits. I hugged her tightly.

"I designed this cake because I'm your second mother." She laughed and hugged me tightly back.

I stared at the design one more time, it was Charles' baby handprint inside his now handprint.

I couldn't believe what Susan had created, to say it was amazing was an absolute understatement.

"I will let you carry on; I've got balloons to blow up." I giggled slightly, handing the piece of paper back over to Susan.

I walked back over to see how Adele was coping with wrapping these presents to see she was on the last one.

As I neared the table, I grabbed a bag of multicoloured balloons off a shelf and threw them onto the table.

"Balloon blowing time," I sang at Adele.

"Yay," she cheered, trying to sound excited, which made me laugh inside.

I split open the bag and the balloons escaped all over the table. Adele was the first one of the two of us to pick up a balloon and start blowing. I picked up a bright, vibrant yellow one. At first, the balloon fought with me as I tried to blow the air in, but after a little stretching, it began to inflate.

Adele and I blew about twenty balloons up before we both got carried away and demolished two packs of balloons.

The day had flown by and I looked at the clock that was hung on the kitchen wall and realised that I hadn't offered anyone lunch or a drink.

"Who wants a cup of tea?" I asked Adele and Susan.

"Yes, please," they both said in unison.

"Anyone want anything to eat?" I said grabbing the milk out of the fridge ready to pour.

"I had food before I left, so I am good, thank you for the offer though," Adele replied whilst catching her breath after releasing half the air in her lungs into balloons.

"Susan?"

"I'm good, thank you, honey, I've already eaten."

"OK," I replied before boiling the kettle and making the teas.

"Adele, here's your tea." I placed it next to her on the table whilst she nodded a thank you.

"Susan, this is yours. Wow, Susan, this is amazing."

"Thank you," she said taking the hot tea from my grasp and placing it in her own.

"The cake is amazing." I just stood there in amazement. I couldn't believe what I was seeing, every detail was so precise.

"Anything for my little angel." She looked over at the cake, her eyes beaming with happiness.

It had been over an hour since the cake was finished, the presents wrapped and the balloons all blown up.

Adele, Susan and I were all now sat on the sofa watching TV whilst Charles lay asleep in the middle of the floor on his blanket.

All of us were glued to the TV that we didn't even hear Harrison walk in. He stood in the doorway of the front room staring in amusement at all of us.

"Hello, everyone," he shouted, making Adele, Susan and I all jump out of our skin and waking Charles up.

Harrison stood there, bent over holding his sides in fits of laughter whilst all three of us sent him daggers.

"Harrison you have woken up Charles," I groaned, knowing that Charles hadn't long gone to sleep.

"I'm sorry," he said, still in fits of laughter.

I got up and stood next to Harrison, kissed him lightly on the lips before taking his jacket and hanging it up.

"Something smells good," he said as he smelt the air.

"Susan has made us an amazing cake for Charles," I beamed, excited to show Harrison the wonderful creation.

I took him into the kitchen and opened the fridge door, grabbed out the cake and placed it on the unit beside Harrison.

"Wow, I'm speechless." His jaw dropped to the floor as he saw the cake.

Susan walked in to see what Harrison had said about her cake. She just stood there and watched his gaping mouth as a smile spread from her ear to ear.

"Susan, this honestly is amazing. I didn't know you could bake."

"Well, you know it's my secret talent." She smiled, you could tell she was over the moon about Harrison's approval of the cake.

"All the balloons are done and the presents are wrapped," I said to Harrison, pulling his arm as he went to follow Susan back into the front room.

"What?" he said in a stern tone.

"We need to talk," I replied with the same tone.

"About?" He raised his eyebrow, getting annoyed.

"You know what," I whispered.

"I've just got home from work. Can we do this later?"

"Fine," I mumbled.

About an hour later, Susan and Adele decided to call it a day and left to go home, which then left me with the perfect opportunity to confront Harrison.

I walked Susan and Adele to the front door, where I anxiously waited for them to leave.

Once their cars had driven off down the road and they were both out of sight, I made my way back inside. Shutting the front door, I walked straight into the front room to see Harrison laying across the sofa with Charles on his chest.

I stood in the doorway and coughed to make my presence known. Harrison looked straight at me before throwing his head back in defeat.

"Harrison.," I began to be rudely interrupted.

"I'm busy with work, do you not believe me?" He sat up angrily, putting Charles back on the floor.

"I do." I scrambled for the words to say.

"Do you believe me? Yes or no, Olive? It's not hard to answer." He dragged his hands down his face.

"Yes."

"Yes, what, Olive, you do or you don't?"

"I do believe you. It's just you can't go running off whenever they call you. You can say no." I let the words slip freely from my mouth, feeling the weight lift from my shoulders.

"I know, I'm sorry. Work is chaotic right now." I stood there stunned at what he had just said. I thought he would bite my head off, but he actually agreed with me.

"I'm sorry too, I didn't know how much stress you have been under with work being so busy." I walked over and sat next to him resting my hand on his thigh.

"It's fine, Olive," he said softly.

"I just got scared," I said so innocently.

"Of what?"

"You not wanting me anymore." He grabbed my hand and stroked the back of it with his thumb.

"What do you mean? Why wouldn't I want you anymore?" he asked, turning to face me.

"I thought you might have been cheating on me." I gulped.

As soon as I said those words, I instantly regretted it.

Harrison stood up and towered over me, his fists clenched. "How dare you think that," he burst outraged.

"I'm sorry."

"No, Olive. I have helped you; I was there for you. I would have not stuck by your side for me just to cheat on you." The anger was clearly visible on his face as it got redder and redder.

"I know, I'm sorry. I wasn't thinking straight." Tears spilt down my cheeks and Charles began to cry.

Harrison looked over at the child that lay on the floor, picked him up and cradled him. Every now and then, you could hear him whisper 'sorry buddy'.

I ran out of the room and up the stairs. I locked myself in the bathroom after slamming the door shut. Sliding down the back of the bathroom door, I could hear Harrison shouting my name and 'I'm sorry 'or 'I didn't mean it'.

I just sat there my head lay between my knees. I could hear Harrison's footsteps coming up the stairs.

I closed my eyes, kept them shut tightly as he came to halt right outside the bathroom door.

Harrison slightly knocked on the bathroom door. He knocked countless times before giving up and sitting down outside. "Olive, please come out. I'm sorry. Olive, I didn't mean it. I know you have been through a lot, Olive. I was out of line. I love you," he said, but you could hear through the tone of his voice that he was holding back the tears.

I just sat there in silence listening to Harrison speaking soft words to me, trying everything he could to get me to come out.

"Olive, please come out."

It wasn't long until Harrison gave up and I could hear him stand up and his footsteps fade away.

It had been over two hours, so I decided to get up and take a shower. I pulled my phone from my pocket to check the time to see it was nearly 10 o'clock.

I turned the shower on, watching the steam rise as the heat in the water became stronger. The hot water hit my skin as I stood under the showerhead. I let my head relax back, the water falling through each strand of hair.

The water washed away the tear stains from the previous tears and collided with the new ones that had formed.

I stood under the gushing water for at least twenty minutes just processing the thoughts of the day before I began to wash my body.

Once I had showered, I got out and made my way across the landing looking over at Charles' room to see he was fast asleep in his cot.

Then I entered my bedroom to see no sight of Harrison. I thought nothing of it and continued to get dry and dressed. Once I got dressed, I decided I was going to apologise to Harrison and that I just wanted to be in his arms.

I walked downstairs to see the light from the television glaring across the back wall of the front room.

Walking into the front room I saw Harrison's body sprawled across the sofa, a blanket lightly covering his lower body and his head resting on a single pillow.

I made my way over to his sleeping body and kissed his forehead before whispering goodnight and heading back up the stairs to my bedroom.

I sat on my bed and placed my head back into the old comfort of my pillows. I turned to my side, brushed my arm over Harrison's side of the bed when something touched my hand.

I grabbed the piece of paper that was on the bed covers and flicked on the bedside lamp and began to read the words that lay upon the page.

'Olive,

I know you are annoyed at me for spending most of my free time at work, but things have been chaotic and I realise what a toll it had taken on us. Tomorrow is a new day and I plan to make a change. I want to be at home more and I will. I'm sorry I shouted at you; I hope you can forgive me.

Harrison x'

I smiled at the note like a complete idiot. I knew that seeing that note, I could sleep without feeling awkward.

I'm so happy I met Harrison, just not the way I did.

After five minutes, I convinced myself to sleep as my precious little boy turns one tomorrow. Instead of crying myself to sleep, I drifted off to sleep with a huge smile present.

The morning sun filled my bedroom and the sound of Charles' laughter filled the walls of this happy home.

I pulled myself out of bed, got dressed and went downstairs to the front room, where the laughter of my son become louder.

"Happy birthday, Charles," Harrison sang at the top of his lungs.

"When your mummy comes down, we can open some presents." I froze and realised I didn't set an alarm before going to bed to wake up and set everything up.

I walked into the front room to see banners strung over picture frames and balloons taking up the floor.

"Speaking of the devil," Harrison said and handed Charles to me.

"Harrison, this is amazing." I stared at the room in awe.

"It's nothing," he said snaking his arms around my waist.

"Happy birthday, baby." I kissed the top of Charles' head before moving a bunch of balloons from the sofa so that I could sit down.

I sat on the sofa with Charles on my lap whilst Harrison went over to the corner of the room next to the TV and collected the presents. He lay them on the floor next to my feet and took a seat next to Charles and me.

First Harrison picked up a large box-shaped present and placed it in-between our bodies. I placed Charles close to the present and peeled back a corner so that Charles could start to unwrap.

Charles pulled the wrapping paper to shreds, his tiny fingers getting closer to revealing what was hidden.

"I wonder what it is?" Harrison said, helping Charles finish taking the wrapping paper off.

Once the wrapping was completely off, a baby train set was revealed. Charles' eyes widened at the sight of his new toy and happy baby noises soon followed.

"I think you like that present," I beamed, feeling satisfied that I had got something he liked.

After Charles had unwrapped all his presents and Harrison helped him open his cards, I got up, placed Charles on the floor to play and went to the kitchen to start preparing for his birthday party.

I walked to the bottom of the kitchen, where I started to decorate the table. Whilst I was placing a bright blue cloth over the table, I heard Harrison's footsteps coming up behind me.

"I'm sorry about last night," he said into my ear whilst holding my waist before giving me a quick squeeze then letting go of me.

"I forgive you and I'm sorry too." I turned around to face him, wrapping my arms around his neck.

"You have nothing to be sorry for," he said before kissing me softly.

I removed my arms from around his neck and walked over to the fridge and got different foods out and placed them onto the side.

"I need to call Susan, she said she was going to help with the food." I took my phone from my back pocket.

"OK. Well, before you call her and start the food, why don't you go get some pictures of Charles before everyone arrives." I just nodded in response before heading back into the front room.

I sat on the floor next to Charles and I put a small badge that came with one of his cards on his sweatshirt. I sat him upright and made stupid faces behind my phone so I could snap a picture of him smiling. He smiled and I snapped the picture. I just stared at the picture and happy tears appeared at the corners of my eyes. I couldn't believe my little baby wasn't so little anymore. I took a few more pictures and played with Charles a little before dialling Susan's number.

"Hello?" Susan's voice sounded from the other end of the phone.

"Hey, Susan, it's Olive."

"Hey, Olive. Everything OK?" Her voice kind of muffled due to her eating something.

"I was wondering if I could take you up on that offer about helping me with setting up the food and stuff?"

"Yes, of course, honey. I shall leave now; I won't be long."

Then she ended the call, I sighed and looked over at the happy baby who was simply giggling at his toys. I left Charles to play with his toys so I could tell Harrison that Susan was coming around soon, but as I neared the kitchen door, I heard him speaking to someone on the phone.

"God, I can't meet you today. Why, because I can't, OK."

Thoughts raced through my mind, whom could he be meeting today?

"I can see you tomorrow at the same place. Yes, at the cafe." I was confused, I didn't understand.

"She won't find out. I couldn't do that to Olive…Fine but this is the last time." They hung up the phone and I turned and walked back into the living room. My blood boiled; I couldn't believe what I heard.

I tried to convince myself that what I was thinking and feeling was a misunderstanding to what I had heard, but the doubt laid low in my mind.

After about ten minutes I decided to go back into the kitchen.

"Hey, did you call Susan?"

"Yes," I said with a dead beat tone.

"You all right?" he asked, closing the gap between us.

"I'm fine," I said, playing it cool. I told myself I would deal with him later because today is going to be special.

Twenty minutes had passed and there was a knock at the door. I knew it was Susan so I just opened the door and she walked straight in.

First, I let her go and see Charles as I knew she wanted to have some time with him and give him his presents. We all went into the front room and I watched as Susan sat on the floor and handed my blue-eyed baby his presents.

"Here you go," Susan said through her wide smile.

She handed Charles a small box and looked over at me smiling with her eyes. Charles didn't know what to do with the present, he just shook it in his hands.

I knelt beside Charles and took the box out of his hands. Opening the box, I saw a small silver bracelet. It had engraved on it a date of my mum's passing, Ethan and Charles' date of birth with the words that read,' The Three Angels'.

I held the bracelet in my hands before letting slight tears roll over the bridge of my nose and putting the small bracelet on Charles' wrist.

"Thank you." I embraced Susan in a well-deserved hug.

"It was nothing." She sighed, hugging me back.

Time flew and before I knew it, family and friends were arriving. I didn't have many friends but Harrison had a few and my mum always said the more the merrier.

Harrison actually helped with preparing the party food. It was nice him getting involved because over the last few weeks, he had become distant.

"Hi, come in," I said, opening the front door to let in the guests. It had been over an hour since Charles' little party started in full swing.

I led everyone into the kitchen, but just as I was about to follow them, there was one last knock at the door and this is where everything changed.

"Olive, have you got the door?" Harrison came out of the front room with Charles in his arms.

"Yeah," I said, opening the front door.

"Officer?" I asked totally confused as to why the officer who escorted me to the police station was at my front door.

"Jacob, I thought I recognised your voice," Harrison said whilst opening the front door wider.

"Long-time no see, thanks for the invite," Jacob said, walking in and cleaning his well-polished shoes on the matt.

I watched as Harrison and Jacob walked into the kitchen, both in deep conversation. I stood there trying to piece together how I knew him and where I knew him from because I know he escorted me to the police station, but I also recognised him from somewhere else.

Flashback

I was shoved into the back of a police car, my breathing was heavy while tears blurred my vision. I felt so insecure.

I let my hands fall into my lap, my fingertips were trembling. The tears that I was fighting back burst and I couldn't control them, they spilt over the rims of my eyes.

I began to breath faster and faster, making my head feel light, I felt like I was going to pass out.

"We are going to take her to the station for more questioning," the officer said before turning around and glancing at me, Jacob.

I watched as he stared at me intensely like his eyes were burning a hole through my soul.

I stared back…then I remembered he was the officer who walked towards me in my dream.

The last thing I remembered before I blacked out was Tyler holding onto Charles, tears flooding down her cheeks. Then it all went black.

End of Flashback

I stopped with my back against the wall, my breathing hitched as I remembered the dream, my vision playing memories right in front of me as the realisation of Jacob being at the scene of Ethan's death sunk in.

After I got myself together, I walked into the kitchen to see everyone talking amongst themselves and they all seemed to be enjoying the party.

I walked over to Susan, Adele and Harrison.

"Where have you been? Are you OK? You stood in the hallway for like ten minutes, it was like you were in some kind of trance," Harrison said softly grabbing my wrist.

"I'm fine, I will tell you after."

"Cake time," Susan whispered in my ear and I watched as she walked over revealing the cake.

"Everyone, can I have your attention please," Susan said loudly, getting the attention of everyone in the room.

"It is time to sing happy birthday." She lit the candle.

"1, 2, 3." Then she began to sing and the crowd of people in my kitchen joined in. Harrison passed Charles into my arms so that I could share the moment with him.

Susan carried the cake across the room, and the voices of people who came filled the house.

Charles' eyes lit up as the cake caught his attention. Everyone came to the end of the song, and I helped Charles blow out the candle.

Cheers filled the room and Charles giggled, then the cake was cut, it all happened so fast.

Hours went by and everyone was spread between the kitchen and the living room. I was sat on the sofa, holding a sleeping Charles in my arms; whilst Susan and Adele gossiped about their days and Harrison was in the kitchen talking to Jacob.

"Susan, if anyone asks where I am, can you tell them I'm putting Charles to bed?" I asked, tapping her shoulder to get her attention.

"Yeah, sure." She nodded before getting straight back into her conversation with Adele.

I got up from the sofa and walked upstairs, trying not to make too much movement because Charles had been sensitive lately.

Finally, I reached Charles' bedroom, but just as I was placing him down in his cot, I heard voices from the back room. The voice was male and after I let my ears adjust to the voices for a few seconds, I recognised the voices to be Harrison and Jacob's.

Once I was sure that Charles was settled, I couldn't help myself and walked quietly over to the backroom and pressed my ear flat to the door.

"Harrison, you need to tell her. She deserves to know." Jacob had the sound of guilt straining through his words as he spoke.

"I know, I just don't want to hurt her and she already knows my past with Tyler."

"She will work it out before long. You need to be faithful. Olive has gone through a lot," Jacob said, reassuring Harrison that it was the right thing to do.

"I will tell her—" Harrison stopped mid-sentence as a sob escaped my lips. He heard me.

"Someone heard us. Look you need to clean this up," Jacob said whilst I watched the handle on the door being pushed down.

I quickly moved, making my way down the stairs, my heart was pounding. I felt like a mug, I knew he was cheating on me and I saw it but played the fool.

About five minutes after I had come back downstairs, I saw Harrison and Jacob come down, they both had beers in their hands.

Harrison came and sat next to me on the sofa whilst Jacob went and started talking to a woman in the kitchen.

"Hey," he said, kissing my temple.

"Hi," I said, my voice was dead.

"You OK?"

"Yeah," I replied not wanting to do this while everyone was here and on my son's first birthday.

Everyone had a drink in their hands and I was watching the clock. I couldn't wait for everyone to go home, so I could go to sleep. This day had been a bad day and I kept telling myself it couldn't get any worse until Adele walked in the front room, where I sat completely zoned out in thoughts. The inspector and four officers followed in behind her.

The sound of laughter that filled the house had now died and the inspector made his way over to me. Adele had an indescribable emotion spread across her face.

"Good evening, Olive," the inspector said, motioning for the other officers who accompanied him to look through the house.

"Is Harrison James living at this address with you?" I was confused as to why he would be asking that about Harrison.

"Yes."

"And is Susan Davies here this evening?" I looked over my shoulder towards Susan and sent her a confusing look.

"Yes, sir, she is right there." I pointed and Susan walked over and stood right in front of the inspector.

"Is Jessica Davies here too?" I remembered seeing Jessica when I let a group of people in, but we hadn't spoken yet.

"I think she is here." As I said those words, she walked into the front room with a glass of wine in one hand and her phone glued to her other.

"Olive, sorry, I haven't spoken. I've been catching up with some old school friends, so I thought I'd come to see how you are doing now before I leave." She paused as she looked up from her phone to see everyone staring at her.

"Inspector?" she questioned.

The inspector stood up, looked around the house and then radioed for his officers to come back into the front room. One officer came into the front room with Harrison in handcuffs.

"Olive, Susan, Jessica and Harrison, I will be taking you all to the station right away as we have a lead into the investigation of Ethan Davies 'murder." The room filled with shocked emotions.

All four of us were told to stay in the front room whilst the officers cleared people from the house.

"Olive, Adele will be looking after Charles, is that OK?" The inspector said, looking over at my dead beat body.

"Yes," was all I managed to say.

The house remained silent, not one of us saying a word to each other, all of us confused about what was happening.

The inspector left the room for five minutes before bringing in a pale-faced Jacob, who was now also handcuffed.

After being left to sit in silence, we were all told to stand up one by one, where we would be led out of the house to a police car.

I was the last one to be escorted out. I watched as the faces of loyal friends stared out the back windows of police cars with not one expression visible on their faces.

"Get in." A female officer pushed my head down and I was yet again placed in the back of a police car.

After minutes of waiting, I watched an officer talking to Adele. I couldn't see what was being said, I could only see the emotion on Adele's face go from concerned to horrified in seconds.

A feeling of wanting to be sick laid at the pit of my stomach and I could feel the walls of my body closing in on me.

The first police car that held Susan in it pulled off followed by the next car and before I knew it, the police car that I was in began to move.

I looked out from the back of the police car to see my home and my precious child fading away again. It was almost like I was caught up in a vicious circle.

The further the car drove away, I lost vision of the house's silhouette. My breathing became heavy again and my lungs felt like they were seconds away from collapsing.

Thoughts drowned my mind. It was like I was reliving a dark nightmare. I shut my eyes tightly and then opened them hoping that this was all a dream and that I was home.

Tears streamed down my face like they had done from the previous months. Everything became too much for me, I just couldn't cope.

My eyes dropped and my mind went blank. I let the silence of the darkness take me.

Chapter Eight

The Killer in a Secret

The room was silent, I placed my arms on the table making a soft pillow for my head. I placed my head on my arms and closed my eyes.

As soon as we had gotten to the police station, all five of us were taken our different ways. Everyone looked so confused.

My eyes started to close and my thoughts had just started to fade, that was until the door opened. In walked the inspector and a female officer, who smiled at me before sitting across the table.

"Olive."

"Inspector," I said, repositioning my body, so I was slumped over the table.

"Why am I here?" I said getting fed up, they had kept me waiting for what felt like hours.

"Well, Olive we have recently found some evidence that could be of use to Ethan's case and possibly close it, finally giving Ethan justice." I let the words sink in slowly.

"I'm sorry, but how do I fit into this?" I asked, leaning my arms on the edge of the table.

"You will find out when you answer these questions."

"I want to know why I'm being dragged in again after I have told you my side of the events that night." I sighed feeling extremely defeated by everything.

"I understand you have, but it's my job and you have to understand this is a protocol to do this and I will be asking you different questions this time." He slid out a little note pad and pen from the pocket of his suit.

"Did you see anyone other than Jessica or Ethan at the premises of the Davies' household?"

"You said you would ask me new questions?" I gritted my teeth feeling slightly aggravated.

"I will, but these questions will all blend in with what I know and what I want to find out." I was utterly confused at what he meant by that.

"Have you interviewed the others?" I spluttered out my thoughts.

"That is not something I can discuss with you at this moment in time. Now if you want to get out of here quickly, then my advice to you would be to answer the questions." I could see the inspector was getting fed up, but I was also in the same boat as him.

"No."

"No what?" The inspector looked up at me after I broke the silence.

"No, I didn't see anyone else there whilst I was there."

"Thank you. Did you know of any other presence?"

"Yes."

"I'm going to need you to explain with more of an answer than yes," he replied, pressing his pen down hard on his note pad in frustration.

"Yes. Tyler, she told me after she came back into my life."

The inspector just stared at my response, then I remembered that I had not come forward with what Tyler told me, but she came to the station.

I was sat there deep in thought about how they didn't know when Tyler had been to the station to tell them the truth that time when I was bought in. She cleared my name.

"Tyler?"

"Yes, Tyler. Did she not come to the police station and clear my name with her witness statement?"

"No?" The inspector looked shocked.

"Then why did you let me go?" I fired back.

"We received an anonymous phone call and there were signs of evidence that weren't let out to members of the public, but the person on the other end of the phone line mentioned certain things, which placed them as a witness at the scene." The inspector's word echoed around my mind as I tried to think straight.

"But—" I started, but the Inspector threw another question at me.

"You said Tyler spoke to you. What did she tell you?"

I stayed silent, realising everything Tyler had told me was not quite the truth, even if there was always truth in her lies.

"She told me that night I was released." I gave a short answer whilst trying to figure out what was going on.

"What did she tell you?" He pressed on.

"She told me she saw me that night at Ethan's house and she knew I wasn't the one who killed Ethan." The words flowed freely from my mouth; no hesitation was needed.

As I spoke, I kept my eyes focused on the clock, which sat perfectly on the wall behind the inspector's head.

"Did she say why she was there?."

"Yes."

"Olive, I have already told you, I need more than just yes or no right now. I need an explanation." He pushed himself upright and lay his hands above the table, his eyes piercing right through me.

"Fine. That night when I was released from here, Tyler, she picked me up and she seemed uptight." I spoke out, feeling the world rise off my shoulders.

"When we got back to my house, I asked Tyler if she wanted to watch a film but she declined. Then she went straight to bed." I watched as the inspector scribbled notes down whilst I spoke.

"She told me about the night Ethan passed. She told me she was there. Then she told me she saw me in Ethan's bedroom."

"And?" He pressed on for the hundredth time.

"She said she saw Ethan covered in blood. He was walking through the front room, then she saw him enter the bedroom and that's all she could remember before she drove off."

The inspector got up from his chair without saying anything. He tapped the female officer on her shoulder indicating her to follow him out of the room.

They had been gone a good twenty minutes, they left me in the room surround by my thoughts.

I had slumped my body back over the table, my arms crossed over to create a soft surface to rest my head upon. I felt my eyes becoming tired, then before I knew it, I had fallen asleep.

"Wake up." A stern voice caught my attention waking me up.

"Sorry," I apologised.

I sat up removing my upper body from the table. The inspector and the female officer sat back down across from me.

"Your story, it checks out," said the inspector.

"My story?" I asked completely annoyed at the words that left his mouth.

"Yes, we traced the phone call back to your house and the user of the phone was Tyler." I couldn't believe that that's the reason they bought me to the police station.

"Is that it?" I asked bitterly.

"No, unfortunately, we have a few suspects and until everything has been cleared up, you will be kept here," he said, his tone of voice becoming harsh due to my recent bitterness.

I sighed heavily, just wanting to leave and get all of this out of the way.

"Follow the officer," the inspector instructed me.

I stood up and walked slowly behind the officer, we went out the door and down a narrow hallway and passed some desks, where I then entered a blank room with chairs that had been spread around.

"You sit over there," the female said with a soft tone before making her way out of the room, leaving me alone in silence again.

I walked over to the chair she told me to sit on and stared at the blank walls that stood proudly around me.

I was just about to get some sleep when the door was swung open and in walked Susan. I just stared at her in confusion. Susan sat in the seat furthest away from me. I opened my mouth to say something but the words stuck to the roof of my mouth.

"What did they ask you?" Susan said, breaking the silence with a straight forward question.

"They asked me if I saw anyone else at the scene of Ethan's death." I lifted my head to see her face.

"What did they ask you?" I said emotionlessly.

"They asked me if I was there."

"Were you?" I raised my eyebrow as confusing and anger burned through the layers of my skin.

"Yes." I didn't answer her. I was too shocked and hurt. Susan had plenty of time to tell me she was there, but she kept it a secret.

"I'm sorry, Olive, I wanted to tell you." Her voice sounded desperate.

"It's fine. I just wish you had told me; I'm fed up of these secrets." I let my head drop into my hands.

The room filled with silence. I sighed heavily before resting my head back and letting my body flop on the chair. It was an understatement to say I was fed up now, I was beyond annoyed.

The door flung open to reveal Jacob, his cheeks were stained from tears that had engraved his skin.

He said nothing, he just sat on a chair in the corner of the room silently crying. I didn't even know this guy other than seeing him in that dream and when I was arrested under the suspicion of Ethan's murder.

Something came over me and I got up from my chair ignoring the guard who stared me down as I walked towards Jacob.

"You all right?" I asked. His teary eyes looked right at mine. I felt the pain he felt just by the way his eyes held a story that looked more like a nightmare.

"I'm fine." He gulped, taking in a large breath before exhaling.

"You don't seem it." I watched as he understood what I was saying, but he just chose not to reply.

"I know I don't know you, but we are all in the same boat. What happened in there?" I rested my hand upon his shoulder.

"I lost my job as an officer over a mistake that I never should have made." I stiffened at his words, realising that he could have been the one who killed Ethan.

"You lost your job?" I carried on, not really caring if he was a murderer. It could be Susan, Jacob, Jessica or Harrison.

"Yeah, I gave false evidence." His eyes darted around the room as he reminisced back to that night.

"Like what?" I said, dragging a chair and sitting next to him.

"I can't say. I've said enough already. I'm sorry you've had to go through this." He placed his hand on top of mine, but I stayed silent.

We all sat there letting the silence contain us again, but this time, I let the thoughts get the better of me and this is when the memories started coming back.

Flashback

Walking into Ethan's house I searched for the light switch but failed to find it on the wall.

"Olive," Ethan said, his voice so soft.

"Sorry, I didn't mean to make that much noise," I apologised as I had knocked over some unknown objects.

"It's OK," he said, flipping the switch on whilst laughing at my clumsy state.

"What do you want to talk about?" he asked and I followed him into the kitchen.

"About my child." He had sad eyes, which clearly hung over his guilt. I stood there and I couldn't say anything, remembering that the last time I bought this subject up, he raged at me.

"Olive, I'm sorry about what happened, I was out of line."

"It's fine, I understand you don't want anything to do with him." I stopped speaking as I realised I had just let slip to Ethan that it was going to be a baby boy.

"It's a boy." The smile on Ethan's face grew wide, it spread from ear to ear. I just stood there with no emotion on my face.

"Olive, what's wrong?" he asked, concern filled his voice.

"You said you don't want anything to do with him."

"I do now," he said, trying so hard to convince me to believe his words.

"Now? Just for now or when he's born?"

"You know what I mean, Olive, I want everything to do with this child." Ethan's words were rudely interrupted by a high-pitched voice, whom I knew to be Jessica's.

"Ethan, Olive, a child," she screamed, her voice bouncing off walls.

I stood there in silence as I listened to Ethan and Jessica argue. I felt so unwanted and disgusted with myself as I realised that I was the reason they were arguing. I was the cause of the pain in their relationship.

End of Flashback

"Olive?" I saw a hand waving in front of my face, completely breaking the trance that I was held up in.

The voice that said my name, I recognised it. I turned my head to the side to see Harrison. He had his arms wide open and I walked straight into them falling into his grasp.

"It's OK." He smoothed my hair as I sobbed into his shoulder.

"What did they ask you?" I removed myself from his embrace, wiping my eyes.

"They asked me if I was there the night of Ethan's passing," he said, guilt instantly appearing over his face.

"Were you?" I asked, already knowing the answer by the way his face twisted as I asked him.

"Umm..." He began before I stood up, fury igniting inside me.

"It's simple, Harrison, yes or no?" He looked around the room, first looking at Jacob, who simply just shook his head. Then he looked over at Susan, who was just as confused as I was.

"Yes, I was there."

I stumbled backwards mumbling to myself.

"This can't be happening." I watched as Harrison came over to me, his voice muffled. He reached out to grab my hand.

"Don't touch me." I moved my hands away, backing away from him. His eyes filled with regret. He took one more look at me before returning to his seat.

Tears fell running down my cheeks. My breathing was heavy, I kept telling myself that nothing else could go wrong but that was far from true.

An hour went by, then the last of us entered the room, Jessica. She took a seat next to Harrison, who just looked at me, guilt drowning his eyes. I watched as Jessica rested her head upon his shoulder and her hands wrapped around his forearm.

My heart pounded out of my chest. I looked Harrison right in the eyes, he just mouthed 'I'm sorry', then the beating of my heart stopped and shattered into a million pieces.

Susan got up from her chair and walked over to me. Her eyes filled with sorrow. She moved a strand of hair that had fallen in front of my face to the side.

"I know." I sobbed harder, releasing years of emotions into Susan's shirt.

The room stayed silent, all that could be heard was the deep, tired sighs that escaped our mouths.

Another hour went by before I was asked to enter another room. My body was tired and I felt like I had drowned in reality.

I took a seat yet again on the other side of the table across from the inspector.

"Sorry to keep you waiting." I nodded my head giving him a lazy response.

"We have got a few more questions we would like to ask you, this won't take long." I didn't even nod in response for the inspector to take the hint and just start with the questioning.

"Olive, how well do you know Jessica?"

"I don't know her that well. I mean I have known her for years. It just depends on why you're asking."

"Did you know that whilst she was with Ethan, she was having an affair?" It was fair to say that before the inspector said those words, I had given up and wasn't completely bothered about being here, but now my head was straight forward and eager.

"No? I always thought she might have been though." The inspector raised his eyebrows, you could see the curiosity spark through his veins.

"What do you mean? You thought she might, what gave off this impression?"

"She would always come home late and I would receive messages from Ethan saying that some nights, she never came home."

"Why was he still with her?"

"I don't know. Honestly, she had this hold on him, I never understood it."

"Next question I have to ask you is about Charles."

"Why do you need to know about Charles? He wasn't even there."

"He was Ethan's, yes?"

"Yes," I said, leaning my elbows on the table.

"Did Jessica start acting strange around the time she knew about Charles being Ethan's?"

"No, she didn't actually know until the night he passed away."

"How did she find out?"

"Well, he asked me to come around and we were talking in the kitchen, then she came home and heard half of the conversation."

"Where did you go after the conversation?"

"Well, Ethan asked me to go to his bedroom, he told me he needed to sort this out, then he motioned between himself and Jessica."

"Is that why you were in the bedroom when we arrived?"

"Yes."

"When you got to the room, do you remember anything unfamiliar?"

"Yes, Ethan had packed all of Jessica's things and there was a note." I stopped mid-sentence, I got lost for a moment.

Flashback

I walked into Ethan's bedroom, guilt sinking in my stomach. I kept telling myself 'my mum never bought me up to ruin a relationship...to become a cheat'.

The yelling from the kitchen bounced through the walls of the family home. I covered my ears and sat on the floor at the end of the bed.

I rocked myself back and forth. The more I could hear the heartache and tragic voices battling with each other, the more I couldn't handle the breaking of my own heart.

The house went silent for a few minutes, then I noticed a load of black bags labelled differently. As I reached down to have a closer look at the bags, my skin caught on a piece of paper that was sat perfectly on top of a bag.

'Dear Jessica,

I have found love, a love that is pure and a love that is loyal. They say that a few arguments help a relationship between loved one's bond, but too many are bad for the heart.

I hate to be the one to do this, but one of us has to grow and make the decision. We aren't meant to be and I'm sorry, it has taken me this long to see what was in front of me all this time.

We shared good memories, but they have been overpowered by the bad. I feel ashamed to have led you this far, but I have secretly been in love with someone else, who has been right in reaching distance all my life, but I have been blinded by denial. I wasn't sure if she felt the same way, but the look in her eyes says it all. Yours sincerely, Ethan.'

I placed the letter back and just as I did, a male voice, whom I did not recognise was added into the conversation. I made my way out of the bedroom and peered into the kitchen to see a tall male.

I walked in making my presence known. The tall figure looked right at me; his eyes buried themselves into my soul.

Next thing I know is a pain shot through the back of my head. I fell to the ground, a pair of arms breaking the harsh impact.

"Why did you do that, you could have killed her Jessica." A muffled voice said, then before I know it, I was picked up and carried, then placed on a bed.

"Stay out of trouble, you're an innocent soul. Don't get tangled up in dark lies," they said before shutting the door. That's when I recognised the unknown voice to be Harrison's.

End of Flashback

"Olive?" The inspector said, the sound of concern evident in his voice.

"Yeah, um, sorry," I stuttered.

"You said there was a note?"

"Yes, to Jessica, he was leaving her." The inspector began writing on his note pad again, leaving me in utter shock at the memory that had flooded back to me.

"One more thing. Can you think really hard if there was anyone else there that night?" I took a deep breath before replying.

"Harrison. I was thinking about the note, then I had a flashback. He was there and Jessica was the one who hit me across the back of the head."

"Thank you, Olive. You can go back to the room now."

"Wait, what? I can't go home yet?" My eyes were heavy and my body was ready to relax.

"I'm sorry, not just yet," he said. I could tell he wanted to say more but he couldn't.

I was then escorted back to the room, all eyes were on me. Taking a seat, I glanced over at Harrison. I couldn't believe how he dug his way into my life, how he became so invested in me knowing everything he knew.

My mind flowed freely through the thoughts and feelings that were contained in the walls of my body.

"Harrison, Inspector Brown would like to see you again," a male officer said.

Harrison just nodded and stood up following the officer out of the room. Jessica was then left to sit on her own, but every now and then, you could see her glancing over at me.

"Jessica, what's your problem?" I spat out, not regretting the tone of voice I used.

"Nothing. Why?" she spat back.

"Stop staring at me, it's childish." She just huffed and held her head in her hands.

I watched as Susan's head bounced back and forth between Jessica and me.

Minutes flew by and Harrison entered the room. His eyes bloodshot, his cheeks a fiery red. All heads turned to him, everyone reading each emotion that he was letting off.

"Jacob, you're next," the officer said, watching Harrison's every move as he took his seat next to Jessica.

Jacob walked slowly out of the room. Every second he would glance back at Harrison, who simply just shook his head in defeat.

Jacob was gone for ages, no one said a word while he was gone. Harrison and Jessica were cuddled up together and Susan and I were left alone.

"I didn't kill, Tyler," Susan said out of nowhere, catching all of us off guard.

"I didn't think you did anyway?" I questioned, not really processing what exactly was going on.

"I was questioned about it. The inspector tore me to pieces," she bellowed, tears streaming from her eyes. The breaking of her heart sounded through her words.

"They thought I poisoned Tyler."

"What? How could they think that?" Tears now beginning to form in my eyes.

"Her autopsy showed that she had been poisoned and that was the cause of death." Hearing those words shattered the walls I had built up. I didn't know what to believe.

"What?" I placed my fingers over my temples rubbing them harshly becoming frustrated.

"But...Why would they think it was you?"

"Because they said she was gradually poisoned over time and because she was living with me prior to living with you. That it was me."

I sat there stunned by this new information.

"You didn't though, did you?" I couldn't trust anyone. I had to be sure. Susan was like a mother to me; she could never do this to me.

"No, I didn't do it…I didn't." Susan cried painfully. She rocked back and forth on her chair. I watched as her breathing became heavy, she looked like she was going to pass out.

I walked over to her, lifted her head and looked her in the eyes. As soon as I saw the strain and the hurt, I knew she didn't do it.

"I didn't do it," Susan repeated. She became very unstable. It pained me to see her like this, it was like the day she lost Ethan all over again.

"I did it." Everyone's head snapped towards Harrison; his voice echoed loudly around the room. No one spoke as shock filled the empty atmosphere.

"I'm sorry, I did it. I couldn't take it anymore. She was always on my back. I had been living with Jessica; I had an affair with Jessica. I told Tyler I was going on a business trip, but Tyler found out where I was. She followed me here." No one in the room could believe the words that just fell so easily from Harrison's mouth.

"She didn't trust me anymore, she made it clear. She saw Jessica and me in town one day, that's when I knew she had followed me." Harrison stopped speaking in hope that someone would speak up so that he didn't have to carry on with his explanation, but no one spoke.

"Olive," he said, looking at me. Guilt poured out in his tears.

"That day at the cafe, when we went for food. I saw Jessica, but I thought she had gone out of town, that's why I went quiet."

"You didn't just go quiet, you went as pale as a sheet and guilt flashed in your eyes," I said, shocked with myself because it was right in front of me all along.

"I'm sorry," was the last thing that was said before everyone fell silent again.

The door opened and in came Jacob, who looked just as battered and bruised as all of us.

"You all will be expected to wait here until further instructions." the officer said extremely loud and clear before closing the door behind him.

Jacob looked nervous. He fiddled with his hands and every now and then, you could see the corner of his mouth twitch.

"I have something to say." Jacob said, after a while of debating with himself, he decided he was going to finally say whatever he wanted to say.

Everyone turned to face him. He stood up, cleared his throat and began speaking.

"I'm sorry. I really am. You all shouldn't have been dragged into this big mess. If I had done my job properly then none of this would have ever happened. Although I'm not saying all of us in here are as innocent to the eye as we think." With that being said, Jacob sat back down, this time looking at little more comfortable.

"I'm sorry, I don't understand," I said. I told myself that whatever he meant or whatever would be said in this room couldn't be any worse than what has already come to light.

"You don't understand what?" he replied, looking nervous again as though he didn't expect anyone to speak up after he spoke.

"You said if you did your job properly?"

"Yes, well, I was at the scene. In fact, I was there before the dispatch call was put in, but I played it off by saying I was on patrol and there was a disturbance."

"I still don't understand, that sort of answers my question, but there is obviously more?"

"There is more."

"Explain?" I towered over him, fed up of everyone lying to me.

"I had a message from Harrison saying that something had gone wrong. When I got to the house, your friend, Ethan, he was badly injured and I panicked. I ran over to his side and saw blood on my own clothing from the contact with his body."

I turned to see Susan had her full attention on what Jacob was saying.

"Ethan looked around the kitchen at Jessica, Harrison and then he looked at me. He looked so scared. He then pulled himself up onto his feet, then walked into the front room. I went to follow him, but I saw someone outside the window."

"Tyler," I said completely interrupting him.

"Yes. I thought it was wiser not to follow him. He was looking for something, but it wasn't in the front room. What he wanted was in his bedroom, that's when it all happened." Jacob stopped speaking and shut his eyes tightly before looking over at Harrison, who just sat there staring blankly back at him.

"What happened to my son?" Susan yelled at the top of her lungs.

"As I went to follow him into the bedroom, I saw police lights. I then remembered I had sent out a call about the disturbance. As soon as I saw the lights, I went out the back of the house and around the side. I told officers that there was someone injured inside, but the scene, it was a mess and dangerous to go in alone, that they needed backup." He looked over at Harrison again but this time looking for Harrison to help him.

"Harrison, you can tell the rest. I can't get myself to do it."

All eyes were now on Harrison and the pressure got to him. He jumped off his chair and punched the wall repeating the words 'all for love'.

Once he had calmed down, he sat back on his chair and controlled his breathing. Then he opened his mouth and began to carry on with the events from that night.

"Once Jacob left to see the police, I followed Ethan…"

"Stop…Wait," Jessica spoke up for the first time since she entered the room.

"You don't have to do this," she said, stroking Harrison's arm.

"Yes, he does," I spat at her, getting fed up with her little flirtatious, innocent act.

"I deserve to know the truth about my son," Susan said, looking Jessica right in the eyes.

"I followed him, he looked so weak and the blood poured from the gash on his head. We had gotten into a fight over Jessica and you, Olive."

"A fight?" I asked, thinking to myself that surely this is not why the farther of my child and my best friend is dead.

"Yes. Jessica told me Ethan would beat her because you would tell Ethan to beat her." My body filled with anger. I walked straight over to her and grabbed her arms and ripped them away from her body, taking her by surprise.

"You are vile," I shouted in her face and watched the fright eat away at her.

"What happened after the fight? Why was he injured?"

"He hit his head on the corner of the dining room table."

I heard Susan howling in pain from behind me.

Hearing her tore me right down the middle.

"Carry on," I whispered, I needed to know.

"I followed him. Then I saw he was heavily bleeding. He walked into the bedroom, he went to reach out for his phone, but then I wrapped my hands around his neck. I could feel his body releasing his soul, then that was it, he collapsed...onto you."

Susan collapsed on the floor; she was screaming. My heart broke into a million pieces. I instantly ran over to her, everyone else looked up, tears leaking down their faces.

"When I saw you, it killed me. I only stayed for a few seconds before running out of the house using the back door, running through loads of fields."

I stared at the man I had learnt to love and trust and now everything added up. He was too nice to me and now I understand why.

I felt sick to the stomach, Ethan's killer was living under my roof.

"I helped Harrison kill Ethan," Jessica chocked out.

"What?" I said, sending daggers across the room towards her.

"I covered his mouth. I watched him die in your arms. After Harrison left, well, I screamed and then the officers ran in and I came through the door shouting at you 'what have you done', so it looked like you had killed Ethan...Sorry."

"Sorry isn't going to cut it, you are both going down for this," I screamed the last bit, anger pulsing through my veins around my body.

"I came back in. I was the officer that came in to attend to Jessica. When she screamed, they sent me in. I vowed for her statement, even though I was the one who came up with the plan to say you were the one who killed Ethan."

I fell back hitting the cold wall. I just stared at everyone. I grabbed Susan and held her in my embrace as I watched their mouths in a slow-motion saying 'I'm sorry'.

Next thing I knew was that the door to the room swung open and in walked multiple officers with inspector brown following behind them.

I stood still holding Susan, her sobs vibrated through my body as she cried into my shoulder.

I watched as the officers handcuffed Jessica, Harrison and Jacob.

"Harrison James, Jessica Davies, you're under arrest of the murder of Ethan Davies. You don't have to say anything, but it may harm your defence if you do not mention when questioned something which you later rely on in court. Anything you do say will be given in evidence." Inspector Brown said clearly before asking the officers to remove them from the room.

"As for you Jacob Coles, you're under arrest of the assistance and falsely given evidence and information of Ethan Davies murder. I know you know what I will say next but by 'law', I have to say it," the inspector said, making sure that his fellow officer got the hint. Then he continued with his arrest.

Once the three of them were taken out of the room, the inspector came back and walked towards Susan and me.

"I'm sorry you had to be put through this." Susan moved away from my embrace and looked at the inspector and smiled.

"Thank you, Inspector. You have done my son justice." Susan smiled her smile that had been gone for so long.

"I would also like to inform you that when you were all put in this room, we watched and listened to you through these cameras."

Susan and I looked at the corners the inspector pointed at and we both smiled in disbelief. How did not one of us notice that there were cameras?

"Smart, you knew they were going to break," I replied, the inspector just stood there with a smug look on his face.

"You are free to go, thank you for your co-operation."

Once those words were let slip from the inspector's mouth, Susan and I walked straight out of the station not bothering to look back.

Camera flashes lit up the night sky like strikes of lightening. The inspector came passed Susan and me and stood at a podium, ushering the news reporters.

"I would like to announce that the justice of Ethan Davies, who was murdered a year ago today, has finally be given. I must ask that his family and close friends are not to be bothered due to everything being raw at this moment in time."

"Who killed him?" A lady with a microphone shoved her hand into the open air of the night.

"News will later be shared about the killer. For now, evidence and information are being logged, thank you for your time. Goodnight."

The crowd rambled on, everyone eager to know more. Susan and I were escorted to these black cars that were parked around the back of the station. Neither one of us hesitated to climb into the vehicles.

I gave Susan a small smile before I watched our cars go separate ways.

I arrived home to see the front room light was on. I walked up to the front door and opened it slowly.

The sound of the TV was silently playing. I walked in to see Adele fast asleep on the sofa, soft snores escaping her lips.

I shook her shoulders and watched her heavy eyes open.

"Olive, are you OK?"

"They caught the killer," I said, smiling from ear to ear.

"That's amazing, Olive, I'm so happy for you. Who was it?"

"In fact, I should say killers because it was Harrison and Jessica." I watched as her face dropped.

"Harrison?"

"Yes. I really think you deserve to know this, but he poisoned Tyler."

Adele fell into my shoulder and let out her tears.

"Thank you, Olive," she whispered before letting go of me and walking out of the living room not saying another word.

I watched out of the window after hearing the front door open and close as Adele got in her car and cried. She sat there a good ten minutes before driving away.

As soon as she went, I walked upstairs and collapsed on my bed, drifting straight off to sleep, feeling peaceful and smiling a smile like I had never smiled before.

The next day I woke up early, cleared out all of Harrison's belongings. Then decided it was finally time to take Charles to see his father.

We arrived at Jackwood cemetery. I grabbed Charles out of his seat and walked across the grass until I reached the place where Ethan's body was laid to rest.

I looked down at the beautiful headstone and noticed something different. Someone had redone his headstone, but they had written something on there, something that touched my heart and healed the emptiness that laid in the pit of my stomach.

It read 'In memory of Ethan Davies, a loving son to Susan, a best friend to Olive and a caring father to his son, Charles Smith'.

Tears overflowed my eyes as I smiled down at my son then back towards where his father was buried.

"This is your daddy. He loves you very much," I said through the warmth of my tears.

"And daddy, this is your little boy Charles."

I was too busy talking to Ethan and Charles that I hadn't even realised that Susan had come up behind me.

"How do you like his new headstone?"

"It's beautiful." Susan came over and wrapped her arms around my shoulders, resting her chin on my head.

We stood there for a while just reminiscing on the good old memories, that will always remain in our hearts and on the pages of photo albums.

Susan left without saying a word, Charles and I stayed so I could say a few more words before leaving his side.

"Ethan, I know I never said it before because I was scared, but I love you and I always will. My heart and soul belongs to you. Your son will never forget who you were, he will grow up to know you and Tyler and cherish you both the way you cherished me."

Happy with everything I had said. I quickly smiled at Charles, who let out a small giggle before heading back to the car feeling satisfied that all had come to an end. Our lives can continue to grow.

Once we arrived home, I placed Charles in his pram and made my way down the beach. It took forever to get to the edge of the water, but when we reached it, I stared across the open waters, feeling a gust of cold air swipe past my face. It felt like Ethan's hands cupping my face as his secrets were shared setting him free from his chains.

I stood there and took in the surroundings. I thought to myself about everything that had happened one last time before clearing my head of the events and mentally throwing them into the past.

I sat down on the sand, placing my finger into Charles' palms and staring into his ocean blue eyes. He was mesmerised by the waves crashing into each other. I smiled to myself knowing this was the fresh start I had been waiting for, a new chapter that was long overdue. "No more dark lies," I whispered, shutting my eyes and letting the gusts of wind take my words into the open and the atmosphere took me away.

The End